Maryse Condé was born and now resides in Guadeloupe, having spent much of her life in Africa. She studied in Paris and gained a doctorate in Comparative Literature from the Sorbonne in 1975, and her first novel *Heremakhonon* was published the following year. Her literary output has continued steadily since then with *Une Saison à Rihata*, 1981, *Segou I*, 1984, *Segou II*, 1985, a volume of short stories *Pays Mêlé* in 1985 and most recently *Moi Tituba, Sorcière*, 1986. This gained Dr Condé wider recognition as a leading contemporary Caribbean writer with the French award *Le Grand Prix Littéraire de la Femme*.

Maryse Condé is married to Richard Philcox, a professional translator, and he has worked on the English language editions of her works: *Heremakhonon*, *Segou I* and *A Season in Rihata*.

MARYSE CONDE

A SEASON
IN RIHATA

TRANSLATED FROM THE FRENCH BY
RICHARD PHILCOX

HEINEMANN

Heinemann International
a division of Heinemann Educational Books Ltd
Halley Court, Jordan Hill, Oxford OX2 8EJ

Heinemann Educational Books Inc
361 Hanover Street, Portsmouth, New Hampshire, 03801, USA

Heinemann Educational Books (Nigeria) Ltd
PMB 5205, Ibadan
Heinemann Kenya Ltd
PO Box 45314, Nairobi, Kenya
Heinemann Educational Boleswa
PO Box 10103, Village Post Office, Gaborone, Botswana
Heinemann Educational Books (Caribbean) Ltd
175 Mountain View Avenue, Kingston 6, Jamaica

LONDON EDINBURGH MELBOURNE SYDNEY
AUCKLAND SINGAPORE MADRID
HARARE ATHENS BOLOGNA

British Library Cataloguing in Publication Data
Condé, Maryse
A season in Rihata.
I. Title   II. Une Saison à Rihata. *English*
843 [F]   PQ3949.2.C65

ISBN 0–435–98832–8

Typeset by Activity Limited, Salisbury, Wiltshire, England
Printed and bound in Great Britain by
Cox & Wyman Ltd, Reading, Berkshire

90 91 92 93 94 95 10 9 8 7 6 5 4 3 2

African terms italicised in the text can be found in the glossary on page 192.

ONE

The house stood somewhat askew in the middle of an immense, unkempt garden that had more guinea grass than actual lawn. A path led from the hedge of bougainvillaea up to the twin flight of front steps which enlaced a torch cactus and a dwarf frangipani between the shaky handrails. It still had a certain touch of grandeur. Twenty years earlier, before independence, it had been built by the local magistrate and his wife, both from Bordeaux and both fond of entertaining. Anything was a good excuse for celebrating: a new official arriving, an old one returning home, going on leave, repatriation for health reasons. When the French left, the house had remained shut for years and had slowly fallen into disrepair. Its architecture was too reminiscent of colonial times for the tastes of the new leaders of the one party's regional secretariat. They preferred to have moorish-style villas built on the plots down by the river outside the small town.

When Zek had arrived in Rihata with his wife Marie-Hélène, his growing family of children and his mother, the house had been hastily reopened, the walls whitewashed, the floors and windows done up and the garden weeded. Later, Zek had been offered more modern, less damp and less uncomfortable quarters. He had always refused them. Like his children, like Marie-Hélène perhaps, he had grown fond of this house which was unique of its kind, like his family.

Christophe was the only one who would have liked to live elsewhere – in a mud hut in the middle of a cluttered compound like some of his school friends; or in a cramped little villa in the civil servants' quarter; or even in the new residential district that the inhabitants of Rihata, who were never hard up for names, had nicknamed the 'Garden of Allah'. He regarded this unusual house as a symbol, a symbol that they were partly foreigners, poorly integrated into a community that put its own people first. Yet Zek had been born here, a son of one of the most illustrious Ngurka families, and his father, Malan, had founded the first union of planters and had become a dignitary in colonial times. The *griots* who gathered in the garden on feast days even traced his ancestors back to Bouraina, the mythical Ngurka hero and a household legend. It was Marie-Hélène who created this uneasiness and even Christophe, who adored her, sometimes felt like hating her for it.

Not that Marie-Hélène was the only one to have been born far from Rihata. The excesses of certain political regimes were driving an increasing number of men and women from their country to Rihata which had become a meeting place for many nationalities.

But she was the only one the market women, the traders in the rue Patrice-Lumumba, and the little date and peanut sellers, called '*Semela*', Ngurka for 'the woman from over there'. The 'over there' was not just written in the colour of her skin or her hair. The inhabitants of Rihata were used to cross-breeding. The French, Lebanese and Greeks had left their quota of light-skinned, curly-haired little half-castes and nobody ostracised them. But there was a whole manner of being that was written into her gestures, attitudes and reactions which disconcerted, intimidated or attracted, depending on the case, and made her stand out as boldly as a birthmark in the middle of the forehead, a club foot or a crippled leg. Christophe was frightened of becoming like her. Every morning he anxiously examined his young mulatto face in the mirror. He too came from 'over there'. From

2

Guadeloupe, through his mother Delphine, Marie-Hélène's sister. From Haiti, through his father, whom he had never known. He would have given anything not to be Zek's nephew, taken in out of kindness after his mother died; anything to be Zek's son, fruit of his loins and his desire and one of the children of this land.

He got up to put a record on the player he had received as a present the night before. It was Christmas which for a number of reasons Christophe hated, as it accentuated his feeling of loneliness. Not only did his school friends, who were mainly Moslem, pay little attention to Christmas, but at home he was the only one Marie-Hélène insisted should go to mass. Although Zek objected very little to anything, and respected his wife's and nephew's beliefs, he forbade his daughters to set foot inside the church. Christophe therefore had to accompany Marie-Hélène to Jacques Abouchar's, the Lebanese trader who was a Roman Catholic like them and at this time of year sold artificial Christmas trees, multi-coloured candles, tinsel and sequins. Marie-Hélène made her choice under the fat man's lecherous gaze. Then Christophe escorted her to midnight mass in the little wooden church where there were fewer than fifty people, and came home to a Christmas Eve dinner that Bolanlé, the boy cook, had left heated up, and which always made him feel sick.

This year things had gone better since Marie-Hélène was almost at the end of her pregnancy and was too tired to bother about a Christmas tree, midnight mass or dinner. She had gone to bed soon after dinner and it was Zek who had brought Christophe his record player, which must have cost a fortune as such things were only available on the black market. Christophe wanted to tell him that at the age of seventeen he was no longer a child and that, knowing the family's finances, he did not want such a present. He hadn't dared and had stammered out his thanks, but Zek could see through him; he knew Christophe well enough to guess what he was thinking. Christophe put on his record and was about to go back to bed when Sia came in. Sia, the eldest daughter of Zek and

Marie-Hélène, was his cousin and two years his junior. She was a solemn, detached teenager who seemed particularly gloomy that morning. She sat down at the foot of the bed biting the nails of her left hand in silence. 'Uncle Madou is coming the day after tomorrow,' she said after a while

'Is he coming to see us?' Christophe asked in surprise.

She shrugged her shoulders. 'No, of course not. He's coming to commemorate the anniversary of the *coup d'état*.'

Zek had a brother, almost ten years his junior, who the previous year had been appointed Minister for Rural Development. The two brothers had not been on speaking terms for some years. Christophe knew that in actual fact their quarrel went back a long way. They were the only sons of Malan who had had four wives and fifteen daughters. Madou was the son of the first wife who had given birth to five daughters in a row, whereas the third wife, Sokambi, unloved by Malan and given him by a family of former servants as a mark of esteem, already had a son by the name of Zek. Zek and Madou had therefore been brought up as rivals, each vying for the attention and affection of their father. Without any apparent effort Madou had won. Other factors, of which Christophe knew nothing, had been grafted on to this initial discord. It had all started years earlier when they were living in N'Daru, the capital, before Zek had asked for his transfer to Rihata, this small town where nothing ever happened.

Christophe looked up at Sia who went on biting her nails. 'Do you think he'll stay with us?'

She raised her eyes. 'Not after what happened between him and Papa!'

In actual fact she did not know any more than Christophe, but she always spoke with a great deal of assurance, implying she knew more than she really did.

He followed her out on to the verandah. All the bedrooms were on the second floor and you could see the pilot rice schemes reaching down to the river where, at this time of year, the waters were still high. You could even make out some small, ragged members of the Sawale tribe poling their reed boats and, on the other bank, the minaret of the Mecoura mosque. Rihata was situated on a promontory of a lazy bend in the river. For this reason, even in the dry season, the vegetation was never parched and dusty as in other parts of the country. The rainy season seemed to linger on in the rich grass, in the leaves of the mango trees and in the blossom of the flame trees which were late producing pods.

Sia hated Rihata and everything about it. She could not understand how her mother, seemingly destined by birth and her intellectual and physical gifts to a brilliant life, could have married her father and followed him to this country where only the eccentricities of its dictator signalled its presence to the outside world. So she took refuge in this house, sometimes turning it into a fairy-tale castle, sometimes into a big West Indian great house complete with old nannies rocking babies in cradles. On this Christmas morning she would have liked to have found a pile of presents at the foot of her bed, and to have her fingers tangled in ribbons, as she pricked herself on the golden pins, her delighted parents looking on. Instead of which there was dead silence. The family was still asleep, except for Sara and Kadi, the fourth and fifth daughters respectively, who were playing at the foot of the front steps. There was Sokambi of course, the grandmother, up at dawn, who was busy with her *pagnes* and dye basins at the bottom of the garden. Zek and Marie-Hélène were locked away in the master bedroom, its ceiling pitted with mould. It was obvious that they no longer loved each other. Come to that, had they ever loved each other ? Why then did they live together? Why did they have so many children? There were six already and a seventh was well on the way.

'Shall we go down to the river?'

She did not exactly jump at Christophe's suggestion, but there were hours to wait until lunch. A kind of bar cum restaurant stood on the river bank, where you could get fruit juice, coca cola and beer and nibble on fresh fried fish. For some time it had been a favourite meeting place for Rihata's bourgeoisie who used to listen to *kora* and *balafon* music far into

5

the night. Then the fashion passed and the owner almost went bankrupt. Nothing ever lasted in Rihata. In this small town enthusiasm was short-lived.

She shrugged her shoulders, indifferently. 'If you like.'

The verandah went round the house like a flimsy footbridge and was shaky in places. She decided to change her *pagne* and while he waited for her Christophe stared at the flat grey river which well before noon would be sparkling in the sun. The river had always fascinated him. He imagined the silent journey of the waters to the delta, to the sea and to America on the other side. Perhaps one day he would have to go away and leave Rihata far behind him.

Sokambi watched Sia and Christophe kiss Sara and Kadi goodbye and then climb astride a moped. She pursed her lips. She thought this moped which Christophe had been given as a birthday present at the beginning of the year shockingly expensive. Why couldn't he be content like everyone else with the Chinese bicycles sold in the state shops? Moreover, she did not like the way her granddaughter perched with no sense of decency on the luggage rack, her skirt hitched up to her thighs. Come to that, she did not like the way her son brought up his children or ran his home. But was he really running it? All the responsibilities and all the decisions were left to Marie-Hélène. If ever a man was dominated by a woman it was Zek, the son she had given birth to over forty years ago. What had these foreign women got? How did they manage to control their husbands? Sokambi recalled the things she had been taught when she was young. Never look your husband straight in the eye, speak to him in a low voice, serve him and continue to serve him and never, never be unfaithful. The word unfaithful was a crime in itself. Who had brought up Marie-Hélène and taught her how to behave?

Sokambi plunged her spoon into the rice pap she always made at about ten o' clock to ease her stomach pains. She was no longer young. She was entering her sixtieth year and whereas she should have been spending her days quietly, as the uncontested mistress of her son's home, she had been consigned to a small house previously used by the servants, where she was living off the earnings of her trade. Yet when Zek had come back after completing his studies she had thought a new life would begin for her. Life in Malan's compound had become unbearable, where she was despised, ignored and regarded as sterile because she had only produced one son, and he had taken his time to come back home.

She bitterly swallowed a mouthful of lukewarm, hardly sweetened rice.

Finally, Zek had returned from Paris ... but with this foreign wife, this West Indian, and this half-caste boy who was the son of his wife's dead sister. In fact Sokambi had nothing against Christophe who was certainly more polite and more respectful towards her than her own granddaughters. What she disapproved of was the place he occupied in Zek's house. An illegitimate son treated like a natural heir. It was true that Marie-Hélène only produced daughters – six already! Would this seventh child finally be a boy? Despite the limited affection she had for her daughter-in-law she could not help murmuring the ritual prayer. If only Allah would grant her a son so that she could go in peace!

If she had hoped for a new life with Zek in N'Daru she had very quickly realised her mistake. On the very first meeting she had seen the contempt in Marie-Hélène's light-brown eyes and had felt it in her attitude. Any attempt to take care of the children, feed them her way or intervene on their behalf had been rejected and once again she had found herself helpless and ignored. She had held out for three or four years because a son is not like fruit you can spit out if you don't like the taste. Then for the sake of peace and quiet she had told Zek she was going back to Asin. Naturally, he had begged her not to. So she had stayed. The following year Madou had returned from his studies in Moscow. He had stayed with his older brother and she had been a powerless bystander in the drama until the departure – or rather the flight – to Rihata. It was here that she had taken up dyeing again, helped by three young girls whom she had brought from Asin. Her trade prospered. She had opened a bank account from which Zek helped himself generously. Six children, a wife who never did a day's work, who got up when the sun was already high in the sky, who never set foot in the kitchen where the boys did what they liked, and who smoked until her fingers were stained yellow. Not surprising he was without a rais by the tenth of each month!

Disgusted, Sokambi swallowed her last mouthful and, getting up, saw Zek coming towards her. Every time she contemplated her son her heart melted with tenderness. What a magnificent figure of a man! Everyone turned their head as he passed. Shouldn't he have been the oasis in her desert? The cool water to slake her thirst? Instead of which he was worrying himself to death and never had a minute's happiness. She called out sharply to one of the girls to bring him a chair as he had forgotten how to crouch on a mat, and while they exchanged long, ritual greetings she tried to guess what had brought him. He seemed extremely worried. She did not dare ask. With his eyes lowered he finally said: 'Madou will be here in two days' time.'

Sokambi remained speechless and then managed to ask: 'Is he coming to see you?'

'No, of course not. He is representing the Government in the ceremonies commemorating the *coup d'état*'.

The gods and the ancestors really do make a mess of things! Madou, who should have been given an exemplary punishment, had been appointed to a high ministerial position and had even married one of the President's younger sisters. Now everyone was kowtowing to him. The line of supplicants was getting longer.

'Is he going to stay with us?' asked Sokambi.

Zek shrugged his shoulders. 'He will probably prefer one of the Party's villas.' His voice was hoarse.

At that moment one of the girls came out of the house carrying a calabash of curdled milk perfumed with fresh mint.

8

As he took it from her she lowered her head and bobbed a curtsey, a very common, traditional gesture of respect which made him feel uncomfortable. Only his servants showed him such respect. What did his own family think of him? His children his wife and, above all, his mother?

Like every only son, he had dreamed of providing for his mother in her old age. He had seen her labour far too long in his father's compound, serving her co-wives, since she was no longer fit to bear children, cooking non-stop and dyeing *pagnes*. He knew what hopes she had placed on the only male child from her womb. Instead of which ...

He looked around him. The house to which he had a sort of perverse attachment. The old Citröen DS 19 which the children and the boys had to push-start each morning. All this summed up his failure. Why hadn't he been a success? It would be too easy to put the blame on Marie-Hélène. A woman never completely forges the destiny of a man.

So here was Madou, coming with the prestige of his new functions. In comparison, the humble manager of one of the Development Bank's agencies would look completely absurd and people would say: 'The younger brother has outshone the older.'

The younger brother had always taken precedence in their father's heart; ever since their childhood when Malan had treated him as a dunce, good for nothing but kicking a football around. When only twelve Madou had worked as his father's secretary when he was home on holiday from the *lycée*. Why humiliate his elder son? Was he paying for something that had happened between Sokambi and Malan? It was the only explanation possible and the deep affection he had for his mother, the only being who belonged to him, was mingled with bitterness. The last time he had seen his brother was at the conference held in N'Daru for the managers of the nationalised bank. His brother's name was already being whispered as likely for a ministerial post. He already lived in the residential district that the inhabitants of N'Daru had nicknamed *Petit Paradis*. He was already riding in a Mercedes with a flag.

As the name of Madou was taboo between them, he had not mentioned this meeting to Marie-Hélène. He had not mentioned the visit either. He had left her asleep – or pretending to be – in the large four-poster bed where the magistrate and his wife used to indulge their fantasies. Forgetting the arguments and misunderstandings of the night before, Zek used to get up every morning full of love and tenderness for his wife, and this faculty to forgive and forget humiliated him. His father had been unbending, treating his wives like children or slaves. He had had no scruples about beating them and sending them home. It was probably this weakness, this lack of drive, which Malan detected very early on in his older son that led to his contempt. For he had, indeed, held Zek in contempt. Zek soon abandoned hope of ever arousing the slightest interest from his father and when he saw him laid out rigid on his funeral mat he had felt a kind of relief. Now that his father was dead and gone perhaps he could start to live. How mistaken he had been! Malan did not stop haunting him. He appeared at every critical moment in his life with Marie-Hélène.

The first time was with Olnel.

The face loomed so close and so lifelike that he could hardly believe they had met seventeen years ago.

Those fabulous years he had spent in Paris stood out in Zek's memory, separate from the rest of his dull life. It was not because of the museums, the exhibitions, the art galleries or the theatres – in short, everything for which the city is famous. It was because of the women. The women! Blondes, brunettes and redheads, there for the taking. He had arrived from N'Daru where he had not exactly shone as a scholar, having twice failed the *baccalauréat*, and been treated by everyone as a country bumpkin. Paris had crowned him king, a noble prince. It was not the dismal Paris he had seen years later, while on a mission, teeming with lumpenproletariat from Senegal and Mali. No, it was the magnificent Paris on the eve of the African independences, when every student could devise a family tree of his own. Zek had not cared a hoot for the political agitation around him. While extremists used to distribute tracts on colonialism and anti-colonialism at the entrance to his business college, he would be carefully brushing his hair in front of the mirror in his hotel bedroom, oblivious to the time when there would be afros, dreadlocks and the 'Black is beautiful' cult. Then he would button up the waistcoat of his three-piece suit, slip on his camel-hair coat and go out hunting. Outside the night clubs, Paris was ghostly pale.

This dream-like existence had vanished abruptly when he met Marie-Hélène, nineteen years old, a second-year political science student and with all the arrogance of the world in her lovely eyes. Zek had seen himself reflected in her gaze – insignificant, absurd and dwarf-like. This alone did not explain the fascination she held for him. It was her liking for abstract ideas which had never once entered his mind: the future of the African continent, the progress of the black man and his place in the world. He had followed her, bewildered, to never-ending meetings in freezing or over-heated meeting halls; on marches all over Paris, he had signed petitions and paid subscriptions. Why hadn't she been content with just being beautiful?

It had been on the way back from one of these meetings, marches or lectures – he could not remember exactly – that they had seen Delphine at a café terrace, with a man. Delphine, Marie-Hélène's younger sister, was less striking than she was but pretty all the same. Her grey eyes and crinkly blonde hair had intrigued Zek. Marie-Hélène had explained she was a 'yellow girl'. 'Don't you have them in Africa?'

The man beside Delphine could have just about passed for handsome. Curly, black hair, a very slightly tanned skin and a flashy moustache. She had introduced him as Olnel, from Haiti.

He had no inkling of the drama which was to follow. There was something artificial in Olnel which, he thought, could not delude Marie-Hélène even though Delphine had been duped. Could so much intelligence and beauty fall for this

11

third-rate Apollo who boasted of his family fortune and his aristocratic origins? And yet Marie-Hélène had preferred this charmer to him. Seventeen years later his suffering remained intact. He looked at his mother and said very quietly: 'I haven't told her yet.'

Her only reply was the look on her wrinkled face. The rigid lines softened and between the deep wrinkles her lips curved into a smile. He knew she was thinking. Of Marie-Hélène, of his behaviour towards her. In a way she was right to disapprove. He did not behave like a man, like an Ngurka. He got up. He ought to have the lawn raked and the mango trees cut as they cast too much shade over the vegetable garden. The tomatoes and the okra were not ripening properly.

He felt old and sad and there was a taste of ashes in his mouth. He went slowly back up to the house. The houseboy was opening the windows while the children were clutching the balustrade, piercing the air with their cries. 'Papa, Papa! Here comes Papa!'

He looked up and smiled at them. But their affectionate familiarity hurt him. His daughters loved him, whereas he would have liked them to fear him. They would jostle each other to climb up on his knees, crumple his *boubou* and pull at his face, while he could remember being with his own father, eyes down and frightened to death. Malan had never held his hand or brushed his cheek. When he had got back from Paris, he had gone to Asin to introduce Sia, Christophe and Marie-Hélène – at the time pregnant with their second daughter, Alix – to Malan. How amazing it had felt to be back in the big compound! In the centre stood the main hut, freshly painted in ochre, and inscribed in blue with verses from the Koran which were indecipherable to him now. His father had been inside, huddled in a folding chair, his skin the colour of mud, the whites of his eyes yellow, spotted with red between his oozing eyelids. He was suffering from a sickness that an army of medicine men could not cure. Zek had sat down, biting the kola nut his father had given him, overcome with pity and tenderness that prevailed over his bitterness. Then

12

had come the words which stifled the immense joy he felt at being there.

'Why did you do it? Why did you marry a white woman?'

He tried to laugh. 'She's not a white woman. She's a West Indian. Her ancestors were the same as ours.'

He had launched into a long explanation about the slave trade and the settlement of Blacks in the Americas. He soon realised that his father was not listening to him, and he had not heard a word. So he stopped and, once again, silence prevailed between them. He had never been back to Asin. He had never seen his father alive again.

Marie-Hélène opened her eyes wondering where she was. Every morning she felt foreign when she woke in this pretentious yet decrepit bedroom with its varnish-flaked chests of drawers and trunks, its threadbare drapes and the smell of must that even the sun could not dispel. Fortunately, at night her dreams bore her away. Far from Rihata. Far from her cramped existence. The more her frustration, her impatience and her moods worked her up to a point where nobody, except for Zek, dared approach her, the more magical her journey. In her travels she had smelled the blossom of the jacaranda tree, tamed imaginary animals that seldom browse on earthly grass and listened to the airs of delicate instruments. She sat up, leaning heavily against her pillow. Where had she gone last night? Probably because it was Christmas, even though nobody cared, she had pushed open the door of a church decorated with baroque bouquets. There had been no one in the pews and yet a muffled clamour of voices had said: 'Come on in!'

She had gone up the centre aisle knowing that at the foot of the altar a present awaited her, a present that would change her entire life. But the altar had receded and she had never reached it. This absurd and simple dream, although strangely fascinating, left her irritated and nervous. She managed to stand up. This extraordinary heaviness in her womb told her that the little stranger inside her had started its descent towards the light. Soon it would make its awesome passage, blinded and suffocating with blood and mucus. Deliverance! Never had a word seemed more appropriate. No pregnancy had been as endless as this seventh and last. Yes, last. The farce had lasted long enough. The floor creaked under her feet. Gripping the furniture as if she were fording a river she moved towards the bathroom. There in front of the big mirror where the magistrate's wife used to put the finishing touches to her curls before going down to receive her guests, she lingered in horror at the sight of her reflection. It was not her distorted belly or her swollen breasts. It was her face. The face of a thirty-seven-year-old woman at the end of her tether, exhausted and rooted in failure and mediocrity. She was still lovely. But a close encounter with madness had emaciated her features and enlarged the circles around her somewhat haggard and feverish eyes. She looked as though she were on the verge of some insane or murderous deed. She started to brush her hair – lovely hair, which had been so admired since she was a child, and which she had inherited from her mother – then slipped on her threadbare dressing gown and went out onto the balcony. The children, who were playing a little way off, stared at her, and tried to guess whether it would be wise to approach her, and having decided the contrary merely greeted her with a 'Hello, *Maman!*'

Marie-Hélène loved her children, of course. But she had no time to devote to them. If she was not careful they would distract her from her sole interest: the disintegration of her life.

She sat down in a rocking chair – one she had not shipped over from the West Indies, but had found in the jumble of furniture that cluttered the twelve rooms of the house, like a familiar face in a hostile crowd. Lowering her eyes, she saw Zek coming up from the bottom of the garden, probably from his mother's. *Miles Gloriosus*! It was the nickname she had given him when they had met in Paris. She had immediately seen through his glibness, joviality and bragging to the kindness and vulnerability – some would say weakness – which lay underneath. Her power over him very quickly went to her head. She had not simply been carried away by her senses, as Olnel claimed with contempt. She saw herself reflected in him. Never would she have so much importance in anybody else's eyes.

She heard him approach, brush off the children who were clinging to him and, out of habit, she offered up her lips. He kissed them absent-mindedly. While he was looking for a chair she saw that he was deeply concerned about something, but felt no inclination to ask questions and even less to console him. After a while he said very quickly: 'Madou will be here the day after tomorrow.'

She remained speechless, then managed to stammer out: 'Here! Why?'

'He's coming to commemorate the *coup d'état*. You know he's a minister now.'

'Did he tell you?'

Zek shook his head. 'No, it was Dawad, the Regional Secretary, who showed me the telegram.'

She could not think of anything to say.

'My mother thinks we ought to get ready to receive him, in case he stays with us,' he continued.

Anything Sokambi suggested made Marie-Hélène shrug her shoulders in derision. She despised her husband's mother because she could not help making comparisons with her own. Her mother's name was Alix des Ruisseaux. She belonged to an old family who had given Guadeloupe a poet whose sonnets appeared in every anthology, and a colonial administrator who had become a Prefect of the Ardèche region after the African independences. Alix had been brought up to respect all the values which make the mulatto class what it is. Unfortunately, in her eighteenth year, she had met Siméon Montlouis, black as could be, whose mother sold black pudding in the market and managed surprisingly to raise three children with the proceeds. Siméon, who had never known his father, was not one of those Blacks with fine features and nice manners whose origins obliterate the colour of their skin. No, he was a rough man with a loud voice, solidly

15

built on enormous feet, a typical nigger through and through. Lawyer by profession, he became part of the local folklore. Stories were told of how he interspersed his speeches in court with juicy anecdotes and addressed the jury in creole in full session. To the disapproval of all, Alix and Siméon had married. For love. But when Marie-Hélène, the eldest daughter, was old enough to understand, the love had long since disappeared. On the one hand, there was this vulgar, complacent man, surrounded by friends, mistresses and offspring, and on the other, a silent, solitary woman. Had they waged battle for the hearts and minds of the children? Or had Siméon never bothered? The fact was that Marie-Hélène and her sister were staunchly behind their mother and her family. Every Friday, after school, grandfather Ruisseaux's Citröen used to draw up to the front of the house and take them to Gourbeyre where the family resided. Marie-Hélène never failed to go to sleep once they had crossed the bridge over the Gabarre, with its smell of mangroves which would, for ever, be associated in her mind with long car journeys and nightfall. Then she would wake up as if by magic in a big mahogany bed. Delphine would be rolled up by her side, and her mother, in a salmon-coloured dressing gown, would exclaim: 'What a beautiful view!' as she opened the shutters onto the hills covered in banana groves. Marie-Hélène had worshipped her mother, and was said to look like her. 'But darker', it was specified, since Alix had an old ivory complexion that reddened in the sun, while her daughter appeared gold-baked in its rays. When Alix had died at the age of fifty, of a sickness that no doctor could diagnose, Marie-Hélène, in a fit, had accused her father of killing her and broke off all relations with him. She had learned through Pierre, her young brother, that he had remarried and had a string of children as young as hers.

Madou was coming!

Marie-Hélène had tried so hard not to think of him that she had ended up forgetting him, or so she thought. Now all she needed was to close her eyes and the past flooded back.

Zek had talked a lot about his young brother, with mixed feelings of affection, bitterness and admiration. But she had never clearly pictured him. And she remembered her surprise at seeing Madou descend from the Ilyshin 18 which had brought him back from Moscow. So different from his older brother! Reserved, cold, aloof, almost disdainful. At the beginning, this had irritated her. So she pretended to ignore him when they came face to face, living as they were under the same roof. Until then, the Government had parachuted the students straight from university into the top jobs, but now the intellectuals began to be mistrusted, especially those trained in the eastern bloc. They were left to simmer in a long purgatory which often turned into hell. Every day, Madou cooled his heels waiting in the corridors of the Ministry of Public Affairs and had to ask Zek to buy his cigarettes and newspapers. You could still get international papers at that time and the press had not been reduced to the one party's single daily, *Falala*, Ngurka for 'liberty with dignity'.

After a six-month siege, Madou finally announced: 'I've been appointed to the Department of Agricultural Planning.'

'As what?'

'As a pen-pusher,' he laughed.

Dawad, the one party's Regional Secretary, re-read for the umpteenth time the telex he had received from the President's Office, announcing the arrival of the Minister for Rural Development for the festivities of 28 December to commemorate the *coup d'état*. It ended: 'Advise Minister's brother, B.A.D. Director.'

Dawad had obeyed and advised Zek, whom he knew well. Although the latter was not one of the town's eminent personalities, who were all associated with the exercise of political power, he nevertheless occupied a special place in society. Everybody respected the affable Zek, so imposing in his ceremonial *boubous*, generous and light-hearted in the tradition of the former chiefs. He was unbeatable at telling jokes in Ngurka, endlessly playing with the subtleties and implications of the language. Even Dawad respected him, although he knew he was not a Party card member and never attended the district committee meetings.

'Advise Minister's brother.' What did that mean exactly? That the Minister was staying at his brother's? That he need not prepare the apartment of honour for visiting dignitaries? The saying goes that whatever the position he has reached a man should never despise his brother's dwelling, however humble it may be. But with all the upheavals in the country you no longer knew how people would behave or according to what criteria. The Whites' ways had got the better of everyone. Traditions were no longer in vogue. At that moment Ibra, one of his assistants in the Cultural division, walked into the office and Dawad handed him the telex.

'You know the Whites' ways, do you think he's going to stay at his brother's?' Dawad asked mockingly.

Ibra shook his head. 'I wouldn't think so. I heard they have quarrelled for good. Don't ask me why. Nobody knows.'

Once this point had been cleared up, others remained pending.

'Do you think we should tell Bwana?'

Bwana provided the pretty girls whenever an eminent person honoured the region with his visit. It was amazing how he managed to find them. There was one to suit all tastes.

Ibra understood why his superior was so perplexed. Appointed just a few months ago, this minister was an unknown factor. He had never got himself talked about and belonged to a generation which had still been at school at the time of Independence. Educated in the eastern bloc, married to one of the President's sisters, he was a string of enigmas. To offer him a woman when he did not want one would irritate him. And not offer him one when he would be expecting it would be a disaster. Dawad and Ibra knew all too well what a mistake could cost. The corridors of the regional secretariat were full of upstarts who were on the look-out for a job or a promotion. Dawad picked up the phone and gave a list of orders to the administrative supervisor.

'And put flowers in all the vases. These new-fangled Africans adore them,' he added as a last-minute recommendation.

Then he laughed to himself over the joke. Ibra, who was looking out of the window, turned round.

'Don't forget the petrol coupons for the drivers. They are leaving this afternoon.'

The drivers were going to the sub-districts to fetch the country folk who would line up at the airport. Dawad pulled out his book of coupons.

'What a farce!'

He looked up at Ibra amazed, thinking he had misheard. Ibra was standing in the middle of the room, his hands in the pockets of his Mao tunic.

'What a farce!' he repeated even more violently.

Then he suddenly left the room.

Dawad remained stupefied. What had he meant? What had he called a farce? The celebration of a military coup that had thrown the country into the hands of a dark dictator, generally termed a revolutionary? The arrival of this minister whose only claim to fame was being in the presidential favour? Dawad had no intention of risking his position. Until now he had been clear-sighted and shrewd. In the conflict between Fily, the first president and historical leader, and Toumany, the second one, recently named 'President for Life', he had been quick to shout 'Long Live Toumany', and had been rewarded with this enviable position by Toumany who had pulled some vague family strings.

Until now he had had an excellent opinion of Ibra. What had he meant? Such an outburst could only imply criticism. He would need watching!

19

TWO

At dinner Marie-Hélène had not been able to swallow a thing. The smell of food had mingled in a nauseous fog and she had had to leave the table. Now that she had withdrawn to her room she stared at the carvings on the ceiling turning over and over the same thought in her head. She would never leave Zek, that she knew. She had thought of doing so a hundred times, only to find herself pregnant or with a baby in her arms the year after. So was it Rihata for ever?

She recalled their arrival in Rihata during that rainy season which had seemed unending, washing away all her hopes and the little energy she had left. Was this to be the setting for her life from now on? This sleepy community, lost in the middle of its rice fields? Pregnant with Adizua, she used to push Alix down to the river which had overflowed its banks, and the women washing their clothes would laugh openly at her. She used to sit on a rock for hours while Alix played with a group of naked children who were fascinated by her clothes. At times, a herd of dull-coated cattle would surround her, stirring up the muddy water under the herdsman's watch. What had she done to deserve this exile? Was she the only one to blame?

At N'Daru she had lived in total solitude.

Despite his poor record as a scholar, Zek had been appointed sales director of one of the new state-owned companies, the Somirex, thanks to the prestige attached to his father's name. But friends high up whispered to him that his future lay elsewhere and he only had to say the word to begin a successful political career. But he had never said the word. He did not frequent the corridors of power, the villas of the up-and-coming and was not to be seen at presidential parties. He had a party card – it was compulsory in his position – but he never attended the district, section or sub-section committee meetings. He preferred to dance in the evenings at the Almany or Sankore to the popular Congolese bands. At the weekend he preferred to go off with his friends and mistresses to one of the thatched cabins on the beach which could be rented for a few rais. And very quickly he acquired the reputation of being irresponsible. Marie-Hélène would have liked an explanation. Why did he behave like this? Was he beginning to see through Fily's hollow speeches like herself, through this primary-school teacher president who while denouncing foreign intervention was surrounded by his French and American advisors? Was he starting, like her, to be revolted by the corruption, the nepotism and the mess? Did he feel, like her, that nothing had changed and that this African-style socialism was merely a trap allowing a handful of men to usurp power? She would have liked an explanation, but they never saw enough of each other to have one. Zek used to get up early and dress in front of the mirror, putting on his embroidered ceremonial *boubous* to which he had taken a renewed liking now that he was back home, and which made him look like a prince. He would brush his hair, cut very short, stick a soft leather bonnet on top, slip on his slippers and disappear. The day went on for ever. Dusk turned into night, thick with the fears of childhood, and Marie-Hélène, turning over and over in her bed, wondered for what she was being punished. He had not promised her this. After the drama that had almost killed her, he had consoled and comforted her. In his eyes she was no longer the guilty party, but the victim. Victim, just like Delphine. Even more pitiful since she had not had the courage to bring it to an end. He used to tell her of Africa, his country, his village. They would go to Asin. He would introduce her to his father, that great old man who had never had confidence in him and with whom he had a bone to pick.

What had gone wrong?

She used to walk the streets of the residential district where nobody ever walked. Her neighbours would greet her graciously while stepping out of their cars, but these greetings subtly kept her at a distance. Why was she excluded? Little did they realise how she and her entire generation had dreamed of Africa, demanding independence like a magnificent birthday cake. What could she do? Cling to the colony of West Indians who got together on the first Sunday of each month to eat *accras* and black pudding, dance the *beguin* and pour out their hatred and lack of understanding for the country they made a living out of? She had not followed Zek for that ...

Then Madou had descended from his Ilyshin 18, exuding style and intelligence. Who could have resisted him?

No, it was not as simple and down-to-earth as that, Marie-Hélène had the courage to admit. Young Madou, whose feelings for Marie-Hélène were held back by his education, had been the instrument of her revenge. She knew better than anyone that Zek was jealous of him, even though he played at being the brotherly, debonair protector. Their father was dead and yet his shadow still loomed over them and kindled their rivalry. To start with, she had had no set plan, merely the intention of playing with both of them. Then she had completely lost control of the situation and had found herself in love. Desperately in love with Madou. Now he was coming back. He would find her pregnant, diminished, old and tired, tired to death. What kind of man had he become? Spoilt? Corrupted by power?

There was a knock at the door. It was Bolanlé who had brought her some herb tea. She sat down carefully on the bed and let the tea burn and cool her throat at the same time. Bolanlé had been in her service since they had come to Rihata and was ready to give his right arm for her. But she did not need that type of affection. Where was Zek? Why didn't he come home? Didn't he realise that he was all she had?

She gave the cup back to Bolanlé and, leaning back, closed her eyes.

He was all she had. He was both her victim and her executioner. He picked her up, soothed and healed her, only to plunge her again to the depths of despair. It was as if he were trying not to make her happy and could only love her when she was at odds with herself, in anguish or at a loss.

At that precise moment Zek was pushing open the door of the *Nuit de Sine* bar. He had had dinner with Zakariah, one of his mistresses, who had cooked him his favourite dish of bitter cassava leaves and smoked fish which he never ate at home. But he had not made love to her. Nowadays, no woman aroused his desire except his own wife. The hollow chatter of his mistress made him think of her silence. Her flippant laughter, of his wife's sadness. Her desire to please, of his wife's hostility and impatience. He was upset by the arrival of his brother. He had caught a passing glimpse of him a year earlier in a crowd of indifferent faces. Now he would have to look at him face to face.

'How are you, boss?'

He smiled at the barman. In the bar, every evening at the same time, he would meet his drinking companions and womanisers whom he would never consider inviting back to his own home. He liked the company of these office clerks and bureaucrats, below his social rank and birth, who laughed obsequiously at his jokes and felt honoured by his presence. They too were an obvious sign of his failure. The owner of the bar was a Senegalese, originating from the Sine Saloum, who had married an Ngurka and settled in Rihata. He had the nobility and ease of his race and sitting down opposite Zek he commented: 'I hear your brother's coming.'

Zek felt that even here he could not escape Madou.

'Is he your elder brother or your younger brother?' he went on.

'My younger brother,' Zek replied hoarsely. 'I was almost ten when he was born.'

'Sometimes it's the younger ones who have the get up and go.'

He had expected this comment. And yet it hurt him.

'He's lucky, this brother of yours ... '

He would have to look him in the face. His dark, somewhat sad face with short, bushy eyebrows. What would be his first expression? Contempt? Triumph? Guilt?

Zek filled up his glass. 'I don't envy him. In our country one day you're a minister, the next you're in jail or in exile. Unless you become a corpse before your time.'

Everyone approved noisily.

'It is strange, though, that they are sending us a minister and a member of the political bureau as well,' someone expressed in surprise.

'What's strange about it?'

'Usually we're deemed the honour of a secretary of state, once even a private secretary.'

Zek went and fetched the peanuts on the counter. A girl, one of the usuals, was perched on a stool. He had made love to her once or twice and it brought back pleasant memories. He smiled. 'Can I offer you something?'

'What do you want to offer me?' she flirted.

He was in no mood for this type of game and cut it short.

'Give her a Heineken,' he said to the barman.

Afraid he might have upset her, he slipped her a few rais on leaving the bar. How many beers would he need tonight to drown his sadness? His whole life loomed up in front of him. First of all his job. He was not cut out to be a bank manager, suffocating in an office. If he had been a Black American or a Brazilian, perhaps he would have become a famous soccer player with his name in the headlines. Nobody had realised what soccer had meant to him. On the sports field he was free from his father's eye, his scolding or, worse, his indifference. The girls clapped their hands when they saw him. That's where he had earned the nickname Zek, meaning lightning, it was a kind of diminutive of his first name, Iziaka.

Madou was coming.

It stirred up so many memories. Olnel, Delphine. The suicide. That year, the winter had been terrible. Paris had

24

become Siberia. Delphine, who had come back from the maternity clinic a week earlier and lain prostrate, had slipped outside at nightfall, despite his pleas. What could her last journey have been like? From the Parc Montsouris to the Pont de Puteaux. In the morning some Arab workers running to catch the first bus had seen a naked arm protruding absurdly from a strange pile of snow on the river bank. Marie-Hélène had clasped her head between her hands and repeated: 'Say it's not my fault.'

Not her fault? Whose fault was it then? Hers. And only hers, even though he had insisted it was not, to console her.

Zek emptied his glass. Soon he would feel better. The world would be whole and glowing. The gossip was in full swing. Every evening his companions would rave against those in power. Deprived of any other method of attack, they would sling mud. One of the group recounted how President Toumany had bedded his own son's fiancée. Another, how the Minister for Foreign Affairs had left his wife after twenty years of marriage for a bit of skirt whom the whole of N'Daru had laid … and Zek began to despise them, simply because he despised himself for being with them. A few weeks earlier, a tract had been placed in full view on his desk at the bank. 'Ten years is long enough.'

He had made enquiries with his secretary who claimed she had seen nobody suspicious. Nobody young. Nobody out of work. Zek had not dared approach his deputy director whose arrogance towards him, his superior, gave him the creeps. This young graduate from an American university had been sent to Rihata to mend his ways after having coveted the same girl as a minister, and ever since his arrival he had behaved like a prince in exile, waiting to regain his throne. So the matter had rested there. When Zek decided to go home it was already late, although not as late as usual. Not even midnight. He crossed the town which was fast asleep, except outside the only cinema where a group of youngsters was hanging about, probably without enough money to buy a drink. And yet he liked this town. It was cut to his size. When he went to N'Daru once a year he was terrified by his former colleagues, their unscrupulous ambition, their ferociousness and their passion to possess. He had never been like that. He had never dreamed of a political career. He had never had any ambition but to be happy. What was happiness? A loving and obedient wife. A growing family. Sincere friends.

He arrived in front of the villa. The Sawale watchman quickly appeared at the gates to open them wide and Zek, who did not like disturbing the old man, slipped him a rais which he accepted with the ritual blessing. He hoped Sokambi would not emerge from her house – which she often did when he came home – not saying a word, but just to remind him that she did not approve of these late homecomings. Deep in thought, he did not see Christophe striding up and down the garden smoking a cigarette. A good thing too! If he had, he would have felt he had to be manly and crack some dirty joke. But Christophe was chaste and that sort of talk was pure torture to him. The girls at the *lycée* fell for his handsome little face, his grey eyes, his light skin and his copper-coloured hair. At weekends, when he danced reggae at the Calao, the young prostitutes would have preferred him to the brutes who took them by force. But he did not even deign to look at them. He had one obsession in mind. As he gradually approached the age when Delphine, his mother, had relinquished her life, he was tortured by the thought of her. Apart from a charming, insignificant face in a few poorly-taken photos, he knew nothing about her. What suffering and despair had made her commit suicide? Marie-Hélène avoided explanations and could not come up with any, whereas Zek's were downright unsatisfactory.

Do you commit suicide at nineteen because a lover refuses to marry you and leaves you? Perhaps. But surely not if you've got a bouncing baby boy. That would mean that the child had meant nothing. Was hated even. Hated by his mother. Christophe shivered. Tears came to his eyes when he thought of himself fast asleep in a cradle, innocent yet guilty.

Then he blamed himself for being soft, and told himself to be a man.

But how can you become a man when you don't know your past? When you don't know where you come from?

Olnel.

Without really knowing why, he had imagined this little-talked-about father as a Hollywood Zapata, and he was glad he had not inherited his fatal charms. Yes, literally fatal, because he had been the cause of Delphine's death. Zek was full of cliché's when he talked about Olnel: 'Don't take it out on him! He was an irresponsible, spoilt brat. Some men, you know, are not made to be fathers.'

Christophe stubbed out his cigarette and sat down on the bottom step of the porch. The moon was finally rising in a thin, feeble crescent. The night thickened with large patches of mist that floated into the town from the river. This was the hour, they said, when the souls of the departed wandered wretchedly, in need of reincarnation.

Who could tell him about Haiti? Marie-Hélène seldom spoke of the West Indies and Guadeloupe. When she did, it was with a sort of ill-feeling about a land where only bitterness, solitude and meanness flourished. Christophe did not let himself be deluded. He had his own picture of things. Green, luxuriant hills. Crystal-clear waterfalls. The sea playing blind man's buff. And rising above everything, the volcano, crouched like an old woman, with a pipe between her teeth.

Et cric?

Et crac?

Men, woman and children with his complexion were clapping their hands in unison. Of course he knew these were brittle clichés which would not stand up to reality. How could he find out more? He placed his head between his hands. Who could tell him? Madou? Confused memories loomed up from his childhood as he recalled that Madou had had close enough links with Marie-Hélène to know all about this past they were hiding from him. But would he agree to talk? And then, on the other hand, was it better not to know? Suddenly, Christophe was frightened.

THREE

A guard walked up the centre aisle of the plane, leant over respectfully and murmured, 'We are going to land, Comrade Minister.'

Madou obediently put out his cigarette, moved his seat into an upright position and fastened his safety belt. All he could see at first through the window was a green sea of rice fields. Then came the black rectangle of the landing strip. He felt like a child who for months on end had never skipped one boring class nor dashed off his stupid homework and then, suddenly, the school had burnt down. During all these years he had been conscious of the wrong that had been done; he had tried to forget Marie-Hélène and wipe the slate clean. Now an assignment was bringing him to Rihata. And he had not even asked fate to lend a hand!

Before independence the South West, of which Rihata was the capital, had been the country's bread basket. Its red rice could be found in every market and was even exported to neighbouring countries. But since then, unfortunately, production had been on the decline, arriving at a point where, increasingly, massive imports of rice from the USA and Thailand had become necessary. Agricultural experts of all nationalities had been flown in, and all had produced voluminous socio-economic studies on the rice plains of the Salémé. Despite this, the region continued to get poorer, lagging even behind the rest of the country, which was not exactly doing brilliantly. Although the Minister for Rural Development, a newly-created post, Madou had not come to Rihata to talk about rice. He got up. One of his assistants took his attaché case so that his hands would be free to greet the crowd. Another quickly brushed out the creases in his tunic. Then the small group headed for the exit. No sooner had Madou stepped outside the aircraft than the noise rose to welcome him. Schoolchildren, arranged in squares, were waving little flags. The women party representatives clapped their hands in unison while the *griottes* wailed and the *balafons* and drums struck up. It never failed to intoxicate Madou. He raised his left fist above his head in the party salute and the noise grew louder.

He knew full well how artificial this impressive show was. The schoolchildren had been forced to attend with their teachers, or otherwise face punishment. Political officials would not risk being found elsewhere if they were intent on keeping their jobs. As for the crowd, it had been brought in by brute force. Yet he couldn't help feeling intoxicated. One word, one command, and he could choose the most beautiful of these women to share his bed. The schoolboy would be punished, the teacher dismissed and the peasant exiled for ever.

He stepped nimbly down the gangway, capitalising upon his youth and agility which were his strong points. He seemed to embody the new race of men who would take over from Toumany and bring back a smile to everybody's faces. The Regional Secretariat's counsellor moved forward. Madou had already met Dawad in the corridors of the President's office. Everyone clicked their heels and chanted, 'Ready for the Revolution, Comrade Minister!'

This parody of military discipline amused him as he knew full well the total administrative and political disorganisation that lay behind it.

'Your brother does not need any introduction, Comrade Minister.'

While everyone was laughing at the joke, he turned round and came face to face with Zek. At forty-three Zek was beginning to put on weight and lose his physical charm. He was acquiring a paunch under his ceremonial *boubou*. His facial features were slackening and his long, well-shaven cheeks drooped like dewlaps. In contrast, Madou felt young, slim and full of energy; then he felt ashamed of his niggardly thoughts.

As there was almost ten years difference between them, Zek and Madou had never shared either work or play. Influenced by a father who made no pretence of his preferences, Madou had soon considered Zek as a person of limited ability and in all ways inferior; although this did not exclude a certain brotherly affection. It was during their life together at N'Daru that the two brothers had got to know each other. Madou had discovered Zek's generosity, his sense of family and, above all, his constant concern not to hurt anybody. He was like a traditional head of the household whose home is always open, who rushes to the help of the needy and who is more concerned with his inferiors than his superiors. Such virtues no longer sufficed in a world full of predators and locusts. And the elder constantly inspired in the younger a kind of irritated pity.

The two brothers grasped each other by the shoulders and the embrace seemed perfectly natural to those around them.

'How is your wife?'

'Just fine. She asked me to say hello.'

Madou hesitated for a split second. 'How is Marie-Hélène?'

'Fine, just fine. She was sorry she couldn't come to meet you. In her condition. She's expecting any day now … '

For a few seconds, Zek took delight in his brother's hurt face. Then Madou pulled himself together and began to laugh. 'Congratulations! How many are you now? Well, I shall be here for the name-giving ceremony.'

All around them the roar of the crowd increased. One of the traditional Ngurka chiefs had been brought in from his province, draped in a heavy woven cloth which resembled a Roman toga. His arms, from shoulder to wrist, were ringed in large, gold bracelets shaped like snakes, caymans and other

30

animals. On his grey mop of hair he wore a crown, decorated with the same motifs, which shook every time the carriers took a step.

The old man stepped down and kneeled in front of Madou, who, with a gracious gesture, signalled him to get up. His face reflected total submission and Zek, in his disgust, would have liked to remind the old man that this young upstart, who could have been his son, had yet to prove his mettle. So much for this new society born out of independence! Sons ruled their fathers, the younger brothers their older. In many cases even woman were taking precedence over men.

'Will you come with us to the reception, Comrade Minister?'

No, he had seen enough. Now that his joy and excitement had been dampened, he turned back to the officials. He had travelled so far, waited, hoped and dreamed for so long, only to find a woman in labour. What a trick fate had played on him!

A few years earlier Madou had just been a charming young man, suffocating in the inertia of the Ministry of Agricultural Planning. Uncertain about his future, he had wondered whether he would not have done better to seek his fortune in another African country. He knew he would never go back to Europe. His chance came when the Yugoslav Minister for Agriculture had been on an official visit and there was nobody to interpret for him. In the ensuing panic someone recollected that Madou had spent some years in the eastern bloc countries, and from then on he was always ordered to the front at receptions. He had been noticed. They had discovered he was loaded with degrees. They recollected he came from a good family since he was one of the sons of Malan, founder of the first planters' union, in other words, a militant anti-colonialist in his own right. Then Toumany, who made it his job to encourage the younger generation, had taken a fancy to him and even gave him the hand of one of his younger sisters in marriage.

Leaving the runway, the procession headed for the airport building. A pretty little girl dressed in the national colours handed Madou a bouquet of flowers tied with a matching ribbon. The cameras clicked away. Madou attempted a smile, but was obsessed by a single thought: Marie-Hélène was pregnant. He was going to find her enormous and exhausted. Fate had really played him a dirty trick. Since it was Dawad who was walking beside him, it was Dawad who received the full brunt of his anger in a sudden command: 'I want to meet all the security officials this afternoon.'

Dawad looked at him in surprise. 'The security officials, Comrade Minister?'

'Didn't I make myself clear or didn't you hear properly, Comrade Secretary?'

The line of gleaming cars turned into the narrow Avenue du President Kennedy. Right at the end of the procession came Ibra who, of course, was not entitled to a Mercedes, but a seat beside the driver of one of the secretariat's Peugeots. When he arrived at the Party Headquarters most of the officials had already gone into the reception room.

It was the usual crowd of Party officials, front-line militants, militia, student district heads and deserving schoolchildren. There were only a few wives. The rest would appear in the evening dressed up to the nines. For the moment, the only women present, apart from those working for the regional authorities, were the 'guides', as they were prudishly called, recruited by Bwana and dressed in sumptuous *boubous* in the Party colours, with their hair finely braided. The choicest morsels! The Minister would be really difficult to please if he could not find one or several, to his liking. But for the time being he was not paying attention to any of them. He was deep in conversation with a small group of men, including Dawad, who signalled to Ibra to come over to be introduced.

Madou gave a derisive little laugh.

'Responsible for cultural activities? How interesting! How do you manage?'

Ibra cleared his throat, angry for letting himself be intimidated. 'Well, we have to make do with very little, Comrade Minister. We have been able to set up a small mobile cinema and have shown a few documentaries and a feature film.'

'Which one?'

'*The Battleship Potemkin*, Comrade Minister.'

'A very fine film indeed. And did our people appreciate it?'

'I think they did. We gave a running commentary.'

Madou laughed outright. Then he drew Ibra away, familiarly, by the arm. 'Tell me about Cuba, Comrade. The Regional Secretary told me that you studied there.'

Ibra selected his words carefully, to try to convey the Cuban hospitality, friendship and solidarity, but Madou interrupted him.

'And what about the women? They say they are the loveliest in the world. I've always dreamed of visiting the West Indies.'

Ibra was careful not to fall into such an obvious trap and stammered: 'Well, I hardly had that much time. I was at the Party school. We had a very busy schedule.'

Madou laughed again, then ordered somewhat drily: 'Make an appointment with my secretary. I want to see you alone. Don't tell anyone. Long live the Revolution!'

He moved off. In his confusion, Ibra did not realise at once that one of the 'guides' was offering him a tray of drinks. He helped himself automatically while she gazed after the Minister and sighed, 'Isn't he handsome?'

Ibra shrugged his shoulders. 'Just because he's a Minister. He's got the same thing between his legs.'

'Yes, and it's not yours I want to see.'

Thereupon she turned her back on him. At that moment his overweight assistant, Panafié, ran up panting. 'Sory refuses to sing.'

'What!'

Sory was the star singer of the instrumental group which was to play that evening at the reception.

'He says he's sick. But his second wife told me the truth. He hasn't been paid for four months. His first wife has just given birth and he hasn't a rais for the name-giving ceremony.'

'Can't we give him an advance?'

'You know very well the latest circular forbids it.'

Ibra felt dispirited, even terrified. He was responsible for cultural activities. If the evening was a failure who would get the blame? Who would lose his job? The only thing to do was to jump into one of the secretariat's Peugeots. But when he arrived at Sory's, the latter had just left, knowing that he was in the right.

Some five months earlier, Dawad had summoned Sory to tell him of the new measures N'Daru had taken to reassess the artist's status. He had been requested from then onwards to keep his dignity and not to compromise his voice for a couple of rais at name-givings and weddings. He was to become part of the ensemble which would play at set times and set places for a monthly salary of forty thousand rais. Forty thousand rais! Sory had never been paid such an amount in all his life. He had accepted with enthusiasm. The ensemble had been set up after a thousand tiresome rehearsals. It had even reached the finals of the last national arts festival. But silver cups, semi-finals, finals and press coverage are not enough to feed a man. Sory had never received a single rais of the promised salary except for the first month's advance. He was scared of meeting the local shopkeeper, who out of pity alone still sold rice to his wives.

Sory lived in the Timbotimbo district. It was a real disgrace; a heap of blackened huts that wallowed in mud as soon as it rained. It was impossible to keep a child in good health. It attracted all the epidemics in the world, one after the other, while brand new jeeps sporting the health inspection emblem, criss-crossed the area. What surprised the inhabitants most was that they never actually stopped anywhere. As he gradually approached the centre of town, decked out for the visit of this wretched minister, Sory's anger increased. No, no and no – he would not sing! Not until he had been paid his four months' salary in full. In the centre of Rihata stood a ten storey building called *Le Tour*. The ground floor housed the Development Bank, which Sory headed for. In his eyes the only man capable of understanding his situation and of helping him constructively, not just with reassuring words, was Zek. He had boundless admiration for Zek. In a world where men humbled themselves at the feet of the mighty, Zek seemed to him the only remaining gentleman. He gave an extended greeting to the janitor dozing behind a table, knowing that people in uniform like him could be crotchety. 'Brother, I want to see the Director.'

The janitor stared at him. 'You got appointment?'

'Don't you worry about that ... Just let me through.'

The janitor jerked his chin, which could have meant anything, and fell back into his state of inertia. Sory nimbly climbed up the fine polished, wooden stairs, lined with green plants, to Zek's office. As luck would have it, the secretary who normally would have asked him to fill out a card with his name (something quite beyond his capability) had gone down to chat with the typing pool. So without more ado he knocked on the managerial door. Zek's office furnishings had cost millions, but to be fair, Zek could not be held responsible. He had replaced a megalomaniac whose expensive tastes and infatuation for young girls had in the end sent him to prison. Zek had never felt at ease in this decor, fit for an American magnate, but had never managed to change it. Despite his bad temper, he smiled at Sory who had attended all his children's name-giving ceremonies and recited Malan's family tree. Zek was a little surprised at Sory's moodiness.

'Boss, did you know my first wife has given birth to another boy?' Sory got quickly to the point.

Zek hastily came out with the ritual congratulations. Sory's expression did not budge an inch.

'Boss did you know I haven't got a grain of rice in the house?'

Once Sory had left, Zek laughed at himself. He could not resist doing a good deed and then basking in the glory. He should have been born two centuries earlier when his ancestors threw gold ingots to the *griots*. He was a born show off. But nowadays who could show off except for those who

35

held political power: ministers, administrators, secretaries and under-secretaries, the whole clique of sycophants secreted by the Party? Only they could afford to offer presents or positions.

Madou. Back came the young face, remodelled with arrogance and just beginning to harden. There had been neither contempt nor triumph when their eyes had first met. Only an affectionate pity, which was probably worse.

Zek felt unable to face Marie-Hélène over lunch. So he went through the half-dozen girls with whom he could eat and spend his siesta. He finally chose Sita. She was an excellent cook, did not talk too much and, above all, she would not be offended if he did not make love to her.

Returning home in a very bad temper, Dawad shouted to his wife Farida who was in the yard having her hair braided for the evening's reception.

'Throw everybody out and come here, I want to speak to you!'

Continuing to curse he went into the bedroom. What did this minister want? It was obvious he had not come to Rihata simply to commemorate the *coup d'état*. They had learnt that the following day he was to go to Farokodoba, a village of no interest, situated right on the frontier. What was he looking for? Something in this man who was too young, too handsome and too sure of himself frightened Dawad. He was used to men who drank, laughed throatily and eyed women lecherously, none of this grousing which always seemed to imply being in the president's confidence. He had no right to meddle in the finances of the Regional Secretariat.

Dawad stretched out on his back and all the alcohol he had drunk welled up in his throat. Farida was taking her time and he yelled for her. She finally ran in with three-quarters of her hair braided.

'Close the door! The Minister's arrival is bad news,' he murmured.

Farida raised her eyes. 'What put that into your head? I'll

make you some tea. You ought to be more careful, you're not as young as you used to be.'

She left the room.

Dawad remained motionless, staring straight through the ceiling. His intuition, refined by fifteen years of intrigue and petty plotting, told him that this minister was in Rihata on a special assignment which could only cause trouble for everyone. But what sort of assignment? And who would know? He could not make out these men from N'Daru with their superior airs and disdainful smiles, as if they belonged to a far finer and far subtler species. For years now his only visit to the capital was for the annual Party secretaries' conference and, once there, his only desire was always to get out, as quickly as he could.

In everyone's opinion N'Daru, the capital, was a cancer in the breast of the nation, which itself was in bad shape. According to the latest population census over a million inhabitants were crammed together there and evil that would chill the blood, flourished. The very thought of men sleeping with men, between the same sheets made Dawad spit out the bitter saliva in his mouth. This Minister was a menace. He symbolised the new generation that would pull the carpet out from under their feet, topple them and empty the coffers. Men speaking the white man's tongue and acting like white men. African in name only. Predators at home in any jungle.

Farida came back with a cup full of yellowish liquid. He took it from her and emptied it with one gulp.

Madou knew that leaving the reception held in his honour early would upset his hosts. But he had been bored and his patience was running out. He stepped outside into the night and saw the Mercedes he had been assigned waiting under a tree. Inawale, the driver he had brought from N'Daru, was asleep at the wheel.

'Wake up, I want you to drive me somewhere,' he said shaking him gently.

Inawale wondered whether the reception was over. It certainly wasn't, judging by the music and voices. But he did not say anything and started the engine. On reaching the road, he decided to ask.

'Where are we going, Boss?'

'To pay a call on my brother's wife.'

Madou had managed to say it. But what a turmoil raged inside him!

Throughout the whole day he had played his role to perfection. Oh, those obsequious bush people dressed up in their Mao uniforms! None of the girls clumsily presented to him was of interest. He hated these command performances and except for Marie-Hélène, women bored him. They always seemed to be hovering between fear and devotion. Two years ago Toumany, who had no time whatsoever for such states of mind, had called him to the President's Office. 'I want you to get married.'

Madou had retorted that you needed two people to get married, whereupon Toumany had presented him with the youngest daughter of the third son of his father's fifth wife, in other words, his youngest sister. She was nineteen, named Mwika, and had fallen immediately in love with him. So why not marry her? What is more, she was pretty. He had had no regrets as she had already given him a son and was pregnant again.

To begin with Rihata had been built along very simple lines. Two rectangular districts had been added to the original village. The first, named Le Plateau after N'Daru, housed administration buildings and businesses; the second, the villas belonging to the colonials. Independence had changed all that. To the left of the village, a new ultra modern residential area had gradually been built up, while the old district was left to the lower grades of civil servants, tradesmen and lacklustre liberal professions.

Zek lived at the extreme limit of the old residential district, about a mile from the last house. For a moment, the car passed into the shadows, darkened by the foliage of the big trees, then the house loomed up, out of place and illuminated, like a ship setting out to sea. It looked like a theatre set and Madou would not have been surprised to have been introduced by a lackey in a wig, bearing a torch. Instead of which, in the headlights, an old man wrapped in a thin blanket hurried to open the gates. Shadows appeared on the balcony and shouts rang out. Madou saw a young boy come running up, his face strangely familiar under his tousled, curly hair. He was sincerely pleased to see him.

'Christophe! How you've grown! You're taller than I am now!'

That did not take very much doing. Unlike Zek, Madou was neither very tall nor very big.

They went up the front steps together and Madou immediately noticed a thousand heart-breaking details.

On the façade the paint was flaking, revealing the stonework behind. Mason wasps had made their nest in the hollow of the cornices which were covered with brownish lumps. The floor of the great sitting room, which opened out onto the verandah, was bumpy in places under the worn mats that had replaced the carpets. The scantily furnished, poorly-lit room had an abandoned untidy air about it which saddened Madou's heart. He thought of the contrast with his own villa.

It was not long before Marie-Hélène came out of one of the adjoining rooms. Her figure was hidden by a threadbare ceremonial *boubou* and he found her face more secretive, more passionate, slightly ravaged, on the verge of destruction, yet so dignified in her expectations and desires that he almost forgot Christophe standing next to him, and the girls of every size begging him with identical eyes to take them in his arms.

'I'm sorry for coming so late,' he stammered. She brushed his conventional apology aside with a wave of the hand, then invited him to sit down. Madou was ashamed. While he was being carried away on a suddenly meaningless wave of power, she was vegetating in semi-poverty. He felt like kneeling in front of her and presenting his apologies. Instead of which he murmured: 'Tell me, tell me everything ... '

She laughed. Her laughter had not changed: light with a touch of mockery.

'What is there to tell? You're the one who has things to tell, for whom things have changed.'

She ran her eyes over him and he sensed the elegance of his clothes, the price of his brown leather shoes and the changes in his appearance.

'I hear you're married now.'

Madou shrugged his shoulders.

'I had to sooner or later. President's orders ... '

She laughed again. 'Lets start at the beginning. Tell me what you are doing in this Government. How could you have accepted?'

He had anticipated this question and had prepared his answer.

'I accepted to be in the Government because it's obvious you can only change things from the inside. Anybody who has tried to act against Toumany from the outside has either been thrown into prison, executed or exiled. They did not have the right method. You have to try and transform the regime from the inside.'

She uttered a sigh which was indicative of what she thought.

He lowered his voice in an attempt to convince her. 'Do you really know why I am in Rihata? I'm going to let you into a secret. I'm actually here to make contacts with Lopez de Arias. Myself and a few others have persuaded Toumany to make a reconciliation.'

Marie-Hélène looked at him in amazement. This was some announcement. Lopez de Arias was President of the neighbouring country which had been a Portuguese colony. He was bent on achieving within his frontiers the very model of a genuine socialist revolution, and had never lost an opportunity to criticise Toumany for disguising a bloody dictatorship under a left-wing phraseology. A reconciliation

40

between the two men!

Madou began pacing up and down. 'Our country must break out of its isolation. It must stop being the shame of Africa.'

Marie-Hélène listened without saying a word. She wondered whether all this fancy talk was not just fabricated as an after-thought, although the reconciliation with Lopez de Arias did seem a worthy project. What was she to make of it all? She knew nothing about the tortuous paths of power. When he fell silent, she said simply: 'Go and greet the old lady. She would never forgive you if you didn't.'

And so it was that Sokambi found herself face to face with the boy who had tortured and ridiculed her son and whom the gods were now rewarding. While murmuring the ritual blessings in a hoarse voice, she couldn't help reminiscing. It had taken her time to wake up to reality and she blamed herself for her carelessness. The rules of Ngurka conduct are very special. They allow the greatest liberties between a wife and her husband's young brother – her other husband, as they say. He can attend to her pleasures, be her obedient knight and her confidant. It is, however, a code of conduct. How could she have ever imagined that it hid something else? That a crime was being committed? If it had happened years earlier before the white man had imposed his soft manners and changed the men into trousered women, they would have stoned the infidel, exiled the incestuous young brother and burnt the hut they had used. Instead of which Zek had given his pardon.

'It's my fault,' he had said.

And he had fled far from mocking eyes, with his wife and his children while questions were being raised as to which of them were really his. Sokambi showed Madou to a carved wooden stool which she reserved for distinguished visitors.

In the meantime, Marie-Hélène was deep in thought. At any other time she would certainly have felt very strongly about seeing Madou. But at present she was too preoccupied with what was going on inside herself, and the voyage her unborn baby was about to make. She instinctively distrusted the political plan he had explained. Despite the incoherence and chaos of her private life, she had kept intact the convictions of her youth when, with Olnel, she had dreamed of a free, proud Africa, charting the course for the West Indies and sweeping Black America in her wake. Almost unawares, she had versed her children in the use of a militant vocabulary with all the risks such use entailed. The worst had happened a few months before when, to mark the tenth anniversary of Toumany's regime, a small red book had been circulated to schools entitled '*Toumanyism*', containing extracts of speeches and thoughts of the President. Marie-Hélène had ridiculed it cruelly and the unfortunate Alix, the second daughter, aged thirteen, had, in all innocence, repeated her words at the *lycée*. Zek had been summoned to the Regional Secretariat. What could he have said to them to smooth out the matter? When he got back he just shrugged his shoulders.

If ever this reconciliation with Lopez de Arias were to take place, would it last? How could an honest leader accept the caprices and crimes of Toumany? What did his country have to gain from an alliance with a country that had been bled white and gone bankrupt? Marie-Hélène gave up trying to understand.

At that moment Christophe burst into the room. 'He's coming back. What are we going to give him to drink?'

She smiled. 'That tamarind juice Bolanlé is so good at. It will make a change from the vintage champagne he must have drunk at the reception.'

FOUR

Madou opened his eyes and was faced with a landscape green with rice fields. For a moment he wondered where he was. Then it all came back to him. He was on the road to Farokodoba to meet the envoys of Lopez de Arias. In colonial times, when the region was still the country's breadbasket, Farokodoba had been a prosperous village. It had been built on the banks of the river Salémé, which nobody had then regarded as a boundary with the neighbouring Portuguese colony. The population on both sides used to cross it by boat, by *pirogue*, and by all manners of precarious craft, and would meet at the market on Mondays to haggle over the price of rice. Then the Portuguese and the French had been thrown out. Lopez de Arias and Toumany declared a war of words and posted soldiers to stop any crossings or exchange of money. Families had found themselves separated. Spies had turned up on both sides and were made examples of. Farokodoba had lost all its trade, and the only reason why this small village now had the honour of hosting such negotiations was because it was situated at an equal distance between Rihata and Lulua which, in turn, were not far from the capitals where the two Presidents lived.

Madou tried to gather his thoughts to prepare for the discussions he was going to lead. But all he could think of was Marie-Hélène. He had to get her out of this dismal mediocrity. How selfish he had been not to have thought of her

43

earlier! He would find Zek a job. He was a friend of the Minister of the Interior, connected through his wife to the Minister of Foreign Affairs. Why not a secretary in some embassy? A governor? He had to act, and fast. The Mercedes came to a stop. Pulling himself together, Madou got out in front of the district secretariat, built of concrete and sparsely furnished except for a full-length portrait of Toumany in a general's uniform. The Secretary, a young man with a frightened face, ran up. 'The ferry broke down, Comrade Minister. They've just repaired it. They'll be late.'

Irritated at having got up so early, Madou and his delegation headed for the river. In the distance they could see the ferry advancing with difficulty. Salé, chief of staff and a personal friend of Madou's, summed up the situation. 'At the rate it's going it'll be at least another hour.'

What to do in the meantime? Madou looked around. Some children were playing in the water, shouting. Women up to their waist in water were dip netting. With the young people going to seek their fortune in N'Daru, Farokodoba had been drained of its resources. Madou nostalgically recalled his childhood: the happy bustle of the village, the market, the games and storytelling in the evening. To him it had been a golden epoch. Or else he was lying to himself unconsciously, and this nostalgia was merely indicative of how far he had grown apart from his family. The group returned to the secretariat which was being unsuccessfully cooled with at least half a dozen fans.

Salé, in fact, was wrong. They had not been sitting for more than half an hour when the Secretary, who had stayed to watch from the bank, ran back to announce that the foreign delegation had landed. The head of the delegation, Alvarez-Souza, was of mixed blood and thought it the done thing to sport a Fidel Castro beard, which annoyed Madou. The beard had become more or less the symbol of the regime, together with the khaki military tunic and the unpolished boots. Everyone exchanged embraces and congratulated each other as if they had been long-lost friends. In actual fact,

Alvarez-Souza, staring at Madou, felt a deep dislike for this playboy in a Sanjay Gandhi tunic (Toumany had brought the fashion back from a trip to India) and found his arrogant air offensive. Was it for this that they had fought so bitterly against the Whites?

Still embracing one another, the members of both delegations withdrew into the upper room while the guards – machine guns at the ready – and the subordinates settled in for an inevitably long wait. Taking his seat, Madou asked himself whether he was aware of writing an important page in the history of his country. Not really! For the time being all his senses were on the alert. There was going to be some hard bargaining. Lopez de Arias had already made his conditions known: the liberation of countless political prisoners, including Fily, the former President, who was wasting away on a small island off N'Daru; a lift on the ban on the formation of political parties and on elections. Madou admitted that these demands were justified, and counted on obtaining in exchange technical assistance in the key fields of health, education and agriculture at the lowest possible cost, which would partly rid them of their present dependency on other sources. Through his half-closed eyes he observed Alvarez-Souza's handsome face sweating slightly in the stifling heat and he realised he was dealing with a tough opponent.

Sitting in the room downstairs, Inawale stretched out his long legs. He was used to waiting everywhere for Madou – at political meetings, receptions and his mistresses'. Yet waiting hours in the secretariat was going to be hard. There was no indication that it was beside a river. Not a breath of air. Bottles of water were cooling in buckets, but they must still have been luke warm. Inawale got up, checked his revolver under his tunic and went out. After all, there were enough guards to protect the delegates. He was only a chauffeur. But where was there to go in this sinister place? Having lived in N'Daru for years he was full of the town dweller's contempt for the bush. A group of women frying plantains in palm oil looked up, then started to laugh stupidly. These ridiculous bush women! Shrugging his shoulders he continued on his way.

As Inawale left the secretariat a thin, young man with a pleasant face, dressed in a short, flared tunic, as worn in the north of the country, slipped out from under the verandah where he had been on watch all morning. So as not to draw attention to himself, he was wrapped in jute bags, and those who had noticed him took him for one of the numerous homeless and jobless people sleeping their life away where ever they could. In actual fact, Victor was neither homeless nor jobless. A mission of the highest importance had brought him to Farokodoba.

In a country where the press, the radio and television were muzzled, news circulated surprisingly quickly. Together with his companions in the north, over seven hundred miles from N'Daru, Victor had had wind of the project of reconciliation between Lopez de Arias and Toumany. It seemed incredible. It was as if the hyena, daughter of the night, was to mate with the panther, mother of kings. But since they had obtained the information from reliable sources it had to be taken seriously. Victor had arrived in Farokodoba the day before and had been prowling around the secretariat ever since, waiting for any suspicious signs.

He got up and ran his fingers through his uncombed hair which resembled a fetish child's. To catch up with Inawale, he plunged into a side street bordered with mud houses and courtyards, where women were pounding rice and singing. The two men met at the *Carrefour de la Revolution*. Victor smiled, showing his serrated teeth which gave him the cunning look of a folk tale hare. Inawale did not reply, and was going to continue on his way, when Victor decided to bar his path. 'Tell me what's going on brother? Why all these Mercedes, these jeeps and soldiers?'

'Take my advice. Don't ask questions.'

Victor began to laugh. 'What do you mean don't ask questions. I'm an honest citizen. I may not have a job, but I'm entitled to know what's going on.'

Inawale decided to become threatening. 'Mind your own business.'

If he had intended to frighten Victor it had not worked. Victor began to laugh even more loudly, before continuing on a more pleasant note: 'All right, buy me a cool beer and I won't bother you any more.'

'A cool beer? And where do you expect to find one of those?'

Victor studied Inawale and tried to place him. He must be somebody's bodyguard since he was carrying a gun. But whose? What did it matter anyway? What did he know about the negotiations? Probably not very much. At the most he would know the name of Toumany's envoys. How could he get this information out of him? A beer, he wanted a beer! This type of brute loosens his tongue fairly easily when he drinks one too many. A plan quickly took shape in Victor's mind. With a quick gesture that took Inawale by surprise, Victor put his arm round his shoulders and forced him to walk with him. While they walked, he began to talk. He was an out-of-work primary-school teacher dismissed from the profession. 'Yes, struck off the list! You remember that little red book, *Toumanyism*, they had circulated to the schools? I refused to teach it to my pupils. I was immediately summoned to the Party secretariat and detained for three months without seeing either the sun or my mother. Then I was hit and tortured and struck off the list of professional members, left to wander in poverty like a wretched outcast.'

The more Victor talked, the more uneasy he made Inawale feel. Inawale felt he ought not to be with this man. The things he was saying were dangerous. They were things you only talked about in a low voice, among friends, with the door tightly shut. Inawale would have liked to run off, but the thought of the beer held him back. Finally, he found himself in a narrow alley, a kind of stinking trench, while his companion continued to chatter. They entered a small, square courtyard at the back of which a wretched-looking bar had been set up. A clumsily drawn sign was marked *Au Grand Toit de Médine*. The inside was worse than the outside: dirty, sticky tables, rickety stools, a filthy floor and a pungent smell of urine. The place must surely have been abandoned. Victor clapped his hands. A curtain parted and a real monster of a man appeared – his right eye fogged with a leucoma and a curled upper lip revealing yellow, pointed teeth.

Victor made an effusive introduction. 'Albert meet my brother. But I don't even know your name. Inawale? Ah, a good name, that. I think it means "He who is always welcome". I say "I think" because I'm not an Ngurka like yourself. I bet you guessed that. Albert, bring us two beers. Not local. Heineken. My brother only drinks import.'

Albert gave a wide grin which made him look even more hideous, and disappeared again behind the curtain. When he reappeared he was holding two bottles of Heineken, but Inawale's attention was attracted by something else. Beside him stood a young girl. The country was, of course, full of young girls easily tempted by a few rais. But this one was fit for a king. Inawale studied her beautiful shoulders, shown off to advantage by her cotton blouse which was worn thin, almost transparent, from constant washing; and he savoured the sight of her pointed breasts, which were just as he liked them. While opening the bottles Victor followed Inawale's gaze and said maliciously: 'Comrade Inawale – you call yourselves comrades, don't you? – this is my sister, Teresa.'

'Your sister?'

'My twin sister. We came out of the womb of the same decent, kind-hearted woman. May she rest in peace. I came out first, to see what was going on in this hell on earth where we have to spend so many years. Boys are always more curious and adventurous.'

Inawale realised that Victor was making fun of him, but he did not think of reacting, preoccupied as he was by Teresa. Victor drew him into a corner of the bar.

'Brother, since we are all one big family, I see you'd like to spend a moment alone with my sister, your wife.'

'Would she ... ,' stuttered Inawale.

'She's my sister, your wife.'

48

Thereupon he began talking to the young girl in a language which caught Inawale's attention, as it sounded like the one used by the members of Alvarez-Souza's delegation. His instinct told him again to be careful, and that he was in the company of dangerous individuals. At the same time the beer started to have an effect on his half-empty stomach and the girl was so lovely that he shouted: 'Another round on me!'

And he drew his purse out of his tunic. Deliberately. Because it did not belong to him. Madou, who hated loading himself up with money, entrusted him with enormous sums for paying expenses. Usually, he went about his business with scrupulous honesty, never once thinking of taking a rais for himself.

'Brother, hide your money,' Victor said quietly. 'In this country, where two men out of three go hungry, you could get yourself into trouble.'

'What sort of trouble?'

Without a word Albert stepped out into the back and returned with more bottles. Inawale, who was staring at Teresa, was struck by the glint of hatred and contempt in her eyes.

Teresa shook Inawale by the shoulder. There was no doubt about it – he was asleep. The drug Victor had poured into his glass had worked quickly. She had not even had time to undress. She ran to the door behind which Victor and Albert were waiting for the signal. In truth Teresa did not agree with what was going on and couldn't see the point of it. They had come to Farokodoba on a set mission of the utmost importance for those back at the camp. What had got into Victor to put this oaf to sleep? Would it prevent the negotiations from continuing? Would it prevent Lopez de Arias from betraying them and letting them down?

Ever since she had been old enough to understand, Teresa had been used to war. First of all against the Portuguese. They did not often come to her village, but she was familiar with the freedom fighters and guerrillas who had to be fed and

49

bandaged as best they could, and who talked to the children of a future without the white man and his exploitation. She had been sixteen when independence came and she had gone to the capital for the first time. What a beautiful town Ludundua was! White, studded with majestic trees and overlooking the sea, which she had never seen before. She never tired of walking along the clean, wide avenues which intersected at right angles. In the evening they used to eat cornmeal fritters with minced meat stuffing before going out to dance. She had done a secretarial course in one of the schools recently opened by the Party. And then the war broke out again. She watched Albert and Victor strip Inawale of his purse and gun, passing it from one to the other in mutual admiration, and she felt like shouting her disapproval. Yet she did not dare. It was difficult to stand in Victor's way. He became impatient.

'Hurry up, we have to go back to Muti's.'

Everyone called Kunta 'Muti', which means 'mother' in Ngurka, quite simply because she was so fat that she could have borne all the children in the world. Others said it was the fats she inhaled all day long while cooking. Banfo, her husband, had been one of the country's first freedom fighters hunted by the colonial authorities. He had died just before independence from a badly-treated typhoid fever. Kunta had raised their six children without a complaint. Then, seeing the state of the country, she had slipped quietly into the opposition. She owed Banfo that! Her house, situated in the strategic location of Farokodoba, was a haven for patriots who risked their lives shuttling between the guerrilla warfare in the north, and Lopez de Arias who granted valuable aid in money, arms, medical supplies and instructors. Without Lopez de Arias the guerrillas would never have been able to thrive, and all the patriots worshipped him. Until the announcement of his reconciliation with Toumany.

Teresa, Victor and Albert found Muti in the compound yard, her vast buttocks overlapping a stool. She looked at them in surprise. 'Already!'

Victor then made a point of telling her what had happened

and when he stopped she gaped for a moment and then started to shout: 'Mad, you're mad! And a thief too!'

Victor opened his mouth to protest, but he did not have time.

'Idiot! Who brought you into this world! Ah, you'd have done better to stay out of it!' she screamed more loudly.

She stopped suddenly, looked around her and, getting up with difficulty, beckoned to them to follow her inside. Her voice was low and wheezy.

'Do you realise what you have done? Because of your stupid assault the village will be swarming with soldiers and militia. How can I go on hiding you? How?'

Albert tried to intervene, but she swept away his objections with a wave of the hand.

'You were asked to keep quiet and listen to what those bastards were up to by the river. That's all. What have you got to tell?'

They lowered their heads pitifully. Muti sighed.

'Well I've learnt more than you did without setting foot outside. Lopez de Arias is well and truly going to let you down. He's going to make friends with Toumany.'

Teresa, Victor and Albert stared at her dumbfounded.

'Are you sure?'

She nodded and whispered: 'Sure, but don't ask me why. I don't understand any more than you do.'

A heavy silence filled the room. Teresa was looking at Victor and ached in every part of her body. It was for his sake that she had gone back to war. But this time the enemy had a different colour. The Portuguese had been replaced by Toumany's soldiers. When she met Victor in Ludundua he was a refugee, one of the hordes of peasants and office clerks fleeing Toumany's dictatorship with their entire families. They were huddled into tents at the entrance to the town at the Government's expense. Victor's intelligence and alert mind had got him noticed and he had been given a grant for a mechanics' school. But he had not completed the course. As soon as he had heard of the outbreak of guerrilla warfare in the

51

north, he had decided to join the fighting. Teresa had followed him. She would have followed him to the end of the earth, and that is how she came face to face again with fear, insecurity and death.

Muti broke the silence. 'You can't stay in Farokodoba any longer. Once they have given the alarm, you won't be safe anywhere. Go back to the camp.'

Head lowered, Victor saw himself confessing his failure to his leaders and companions who had chosen him for this difficult assignment. He had to admit he had let himself be distracted from his objective and had not been able to resist the temptation of playing a trick on a dogsbody without getting a scrap of information in return. What a disgrace! How could he look them in the eyes? But Muti was right. In a village where everyone knew everyone else, perhaps someone had noticed them. The first interrogations would lead straight to them.

They listened to Inawale's tale in silence. He did not know how long he had been asleep and had woken up with a horrible taste in his mouth. Nobody thought of blaming him. He had been the victim of a woman and women have no other mission in this world but to cause trouble and lead men astray. Madou, who was conducting the interrogation, interrupted him. 'You say they spoke a foreign language. Which one?'

Inawale became confused. 'I don't know, boss. But it was like the one spoken by the other delegation.'

'Portuguese? Are you sure?'

Inawale got more confused. He was not sure about anything except his shame. Madou looked at Salé, his head of staff, as if to find out his opinion, but he merely shrugged his shoulders.

He then turned to the district secretary. 'Take him to the police station. Put as many men as you need on the job, but find the assailants.'

The secretary hurried out followed by Inawale and his assistants. Madou was worried. It would have looked like an ordinary theft if Inawale had not mentioned the strange fact that his assailants spoke a language similar to Portuguese. At a time when such important negotiations were under way anything was possible. Spies could be around. But spies in whose pay? Moreover, the negotiations had not got off to a good start. Lopez de Arias' envoys had arrived with an unexpected demand for the reinstatement of Yule and the authorisation for him to form an opposition party for future elections. Freeing Fily would not be too difficult – he had been in prison for ten years and was half blind. The old man no longer represented any danger and Toumany could easily be won over. But Yule was different. As Prince of the Bossamas, the country's second largest ethnic group, Yule had been given honours by every government since independence. But they had never managed to get him to accept a post, for however blue his blood, Yule remained a Marxist. An out and out Marxist. Each request was refused with the answer that he would not join forces with a tyrannical, pro-fascist regime. Eight years earlier he had attempted to form an opposition party, denouncing Toumany's crimes in clandestine publications, and had barely escaped assassination before fleeing the country. His prestige was enormous. Students secretly circulated his first book, *Afrique, le temps des chacals* which had become a classic like *L'Afrique Noire est mal partie* by René Dumont. Arias' demand was unthinkable. Toumany would never pardon Yule and let him back into the country. Madou weighed up the terms of the report he would have to write that evening.

Salé, who had gone out, returned brandishing a game of *awele* and joked: 'Come and play with me, Comrade Minister!'

A game of *awele*! Madou had not seen one since he was a child and it reminded him of his father, brows knitted, playing with one of his contemporaries. Sometimes the games lasted far into the night and continued the following day.

He motioned Salé to sit opposite him and joked: 'I don't mind losing. I haven't got a cent to my name.'

'I'll give you credit and I can wait.'

53

Madou instinctively picked up the rules of the game again and they had been playing for a quarter of an hour, while the other delegates yawned and dozed, when there was a tremendous rumpus in the neighbouring room. Finally a guard entered. 'Comrade Minister, there is a man in there who wants to see you. He says it's important.'

Madou looked up. 'Who is it?'

The guard shrugged his shoulders. 'I've never seen him before.'

'Well, bring him in.'

A bony young man entered and ran his eyes over the room with a frightened yet secretly derisive look. He was wearing a dirty yellow, threadbare *boubou* and plastic sandals held together with string laces. In a rough voice he gave the Party salute. 'To the revolution, Comrade Minister.'

'To the revolution, Comrade. What's your name?'

'Imeh, my name is Imeh.'

Then suddenly, without any further ado, he launched into his story and only stopped when he had finished what he had to say. His words made everyone there prick up their ears. They gathered round him in a circle and under a dozen pairs of eyes he started to look guilty.

'Are you sure of what you're saying?'

He nodded. At that moment the district secretary, who had been called to the phone, rushed in. Madou pointed to Imeh. 'Do you know him?'

The secretary nodded. 'Yes, he's a staunch supporter. He comes to all the meetings. His children are in the Party's youth brigade.'

'So we can trust him. Repeat your story.'

Imeh obeyed, this time taking pains to make it stylish. When he stopped, the secretary remained dumbfounded, then stammered, 'Muti, Muti ... '

'Do you know her?'

'Everyone knows Muti.'

'Would it surprise you?'

The secretary stared at Madou despairingly. 'Her late

54

husband was my primary-school teacher.'

'That's not the point! Would it surprise you?'

'Honestly, Comrade Minister, I don't know.'

Madou got up so quickly that he upset the table with the game of *awele* and the guards rushed to pick up the cowries scattered to the four corners of the room. 'Take this man to the police station and get his statement. Arrest Muti as quickly as possible.'

In a single move the entire delegation went out, skirting the secretary who held Imeh by the wrist like a prisoner. Imeh suddenly shook himself free, retraced his steps and stared Madou boldly in the face.

'Aren't you going to give me something to buy my kola?'

Salé chased him out.

'Let's see first if your information is correct. What a nerve!'

'What times we live in! Money, that's all they think about!' sighed one of the delegates.

FIVE

Zek set down his glass of beer and shrugged his shoulders.

'Why attach so much importance to the story? It's a theft, that's all. As for the fellow who gave away an old woman, there's no sense in the story. God knows what he has against her. Perhaps it was merely because she refused him credit one day. They are always giving people away in this country. Sometimes for a bowl of rice.'

Madou shook his head impatiently. It was typical of his brother's trivial nature.

'No, I'm certain there's something more. In any case, I didn't call you in for that.'

The expression 'call in' hurt Zek. He had lost all right to seniority. His younger brother summoned him like a subordinate.

'I saw Marie-Hélène yesterday. She seemed very tired.'

Zek had no intention of discussing Marie-Hélène with Madou, and brusquely interrupted him. 'It's not surprising in her condition.'

'It's not merely her condition.'

The two brothers looked at each other and for Zek the suffering and humiliation of the past came flooding back. The fatal blow had been dealt one Saturday morning. He had danced the night away at the *Sankoré* with Diabi, one of the prettiest girls in N'Daru, and he had been lazing in bed, torn between remorse for Marie-Hélène and savouring the

56

pleasure of the night before, when a boy announced that two of the clan's elders were waiting for him. Their solemn, resolutely ill-at-ease expression had immediately warned him of a calamity. Ngurka society is skilled at devising retribution for any fault or offence. What punishment had it devised in his case? In her distress poor Sokambi had taken matters to the traditional authorities.

Without hurrying, the two elders had given the ritual greetings, while Zek attempted to weave his way through a labyrinth of proverbs, double meanings and clichés and reach the truth.

In the end he had understood.

'I can't believe it.'

'Call him in.'

Only Madou had been implicated. Marie-Hélène did not count. She was only 'the one from over there', capable of anything – as she had proven. Her guilt was of little consequence, unlike that of Madou, and even of Zek himself who had married her, and introduced her into the clan that her evil presence was destroying. Madou had sat down opposite the two elders, a few feet from Zek who could not see his face but only hear his answers.

'Yes. Yes. Yes.'

Had he learned the truth otherwise, by word of mouth or through the couple's indiscretion, Zek would have killed his brother, at least he thought he would have, thereby committing an even worse crime, from which he would never have been purged. The elders had decided otherwise. The two brothers were to remain united, at least in appearances! The innermost secret of the heart would never pass their lips. As for the children, whoever their father might be, they belonged to the clan. The Ngurkas made no distinction between son and nephew, daughter and niece. Only the woman and the illegitimate, half-caste son she had imposed on the household, had to go. Both of them had to go! Back to the swamps where they were born, taking with them the miasmas of fever and corruption they exuded.

He would not leave Marie-Hélène and Christophe. Zek had been adamant on that point. Marie-Hélène had greeted his decision with a kind of indifference as if she had lost her taste for life. Had she loved Madou to that extent? At the thought of it Zek's pain heightened and he felt himself being physically strangled. He suffocated for a moment, then heard Madou say:

'She deserves a better life, a much better life than the one you are giving her. That house … '

'She's never wanted anything different. Can we talk about something else? Her situation is your doing and you want to … ' Madou made an appeasing gesture. 'We're not going to go over that again. I admitted I was to blame and I've paid the price. I'm still paying … '

Zek tried to laugh sarcastically, but it sounded pathetic and desperate. Madou continued as if he were talking to himself: 'Anyway, you came out the winner.'

'Winner?'

'You got her and I didn't.'

Zek stared at his brother and was surprised by his expression. Was he telling the truth? His political power and material wealth did not fully compensate for the loss of a woman? Who would believe that!

Madou got up and moved away as if he were ashamed of his confession.

'What would you say to the job of commercial attaché in an embassy? You've got the right qualifications.'

Zek was so dumbfounded, all he could say was, 'It's impossible. I don't have a Party card any more.'

'That's no problem. We'll find two witnesses to swear that you joined when the new regime came to power, and you forgot to renew your card.'

'And why would you do that for me?'

'It's not for you.'

'She will never accept. You know what she thinks of the regime and those who serve it.'

It was Madou's turn to be hurt.

'You think perhaps I flattered, lied and cheated to succeed. That I even killed when necessary. You're wrong. Everything just came to me. I didn't even have to ask.' And it was probably true. Everything had always just come to him. Their father's affection and consideration. Success at school. Another man's wife. Yes, it was true. Years back at the start of their exile in Rihata, Zek had begged Marie-Hélène: 'I want to know how it happened.'

'It was my fault. He would never have dared.'

Zek dreamt he was hitting Madou until he was unconscious. He imagined the ensuing panic. 'The Minister has been killed!' No, he had to control himself. Somebody else would do it. Patriots would rid the country of Toumany's vermin. Then Zek was ashamed of himself. After all, Madou was his brother. He could see the compound yard at Asin and the small boy who used to cling to his legs, eating a freshly picked mango.

Commercial attaché to an embassy? Mexico City. Where the Olympic Games were held. He had always dreamed of going there. Brown-cheeked Indian women with shiny braids, seated on the pavement, selling apples which were rounder than their babies' cheeks. He would go and listen to the *mariachis* and drown hot *tacos* with great mugs of beer. Why not? Exchange this narrow existence, trying to make ends meet, for a new life so that his children could look to a sunnier future.

Mexico City. Or else Havana. Paradoxically, Toumany was on good terms with Cuba. They would be a stone's throw from Guadeloupe. He had always wanted to visit the West Indies, the places where his wife had grown up and been educated. He looked up at his brother who was watching him. 'She will never agree to ... '

It was a surrender. Madou took it to be so, and gave a little smile of triumph.

'Leave it to me. I've always known how to handle her.'

It was not very diplomatic of him. Once again, Zek, who had almost been won over, was hurt. Yes, he had certainly

59

known how to handle her. Zek wanted to say 'No', but he was trapped. Madou was drawing up plans and explaining:

'As soon as I get back I'll get in touch with Ali Saidou, the Minister of Foreign Affairs. He graduated with me and I'm related to him through my wife. He'll do anything for me. If need be, I'll speak to the President himself.' And, still talking, he led Zek out.

As Zek went down the path bordered with multicoloured hibiscus, he passed one of the regional secretariat's Mercedes and recognised Dawad and Ibra. They were with another man. Giving them a wave, he had the odd feeling of being out of place in his own country and belonging nowhere. Yesterday, his father had fought the colonial powers. Today, his brother exercised the new political power. And what about him? Neither leader nor opponent. Neither privileged nor martyr. So where did he stand?

'I thought those two were not on speaking terms,' Dawad said in surprise.

Ibra shrugged his shoulders.

'Blood runs thicker than water. Two brothers can never be enemies.'

'Even so, I'd like to know what went on between them. You're too young to understand, Comrade, that when you've discovered the mistakes your superiors have made, there's no need to be frightened anymore.'

The third man, whom Zek had not recognised, started to laugh: 'You shouldn't be telling him such things.'

The third man was the head of police who since his nomination a year ago had got the reputation of being incredibly cruel and corrupt. It was rumoured he had been sent to this hole to pay for crimes that had embarrassed even Toumany. He was a fat, debonair man in appearance, who was jovial and made a great show of going to the mosque. The Mercedes stopped at the bottom of the steps and the three men climbed nimbly up. Dawad made the introductions.

'Comrade Minister, here is the Head of Police you wanted to meet.'

Madou beckoned them to come forward and elegantly served a round of whisky. Ibra would have preferred a glass of beer, but did not dare to complain. When the glasses had been filled, Madou sat down and his stare made the head of police feel very ill at ease.

'Did you hear what happened to my driver? I don't trust the police in Farokodoba. They seem lax and incompetent. I want you to take things over and have that Muti woman transferred here.'

The Head of Police laughed: 'It's as good as done. As for Muti, I'll make it my personal responsibility. If she doesn't talk, you can hang me.'

'Don't lay it on too hard!'

The Head of Police laughed again. Men were all pansies nowadays! They wanted the power, but they did not want to get their hands dirty, and they feigned humanitarian scruples. The end justified the means, for God's sake! But he did not say a word, and just nodded.

Marie-Hélène managed to thread her needle. Her sight was going; it was a sign of old age. She usually asked one of the children to do it, but she was alone on the balcony in the mid-afternoon sun. She must finish the little coat she was making. The baby must have something to put on apart from the other children's hand-downs. But she was hardly in a mood to make a layette. She pricked herself and quickly sucked her thumb.

Madou's presence in Rihata was starting to stir up her emotions. He brought back feelings of bitterness, dormant suffering and forgotten resentment. She started thinking about her father. About the hellish life he had forced upon her mother. She had died of unrequited love, of being despised, in body and soul. Alix belonged to a generation of women who never confided in anyone. Least of all in her children. And all Marie-Hélène could do was guess. 'You can buy schooling,' the saying went in Guadeloupe, 'but you can't buy education.' Perhaps they were right; he may have been a lawyer but Siméon liked his rum neat, a good laugh, a coarse joke and uncomplicated sex with the velvet-skinned black girls. So why did he marry Alix?

But more than anything else, she started thinking about Olnel again. She had heard news of him a few years before. Hunting had become very popular among the middle classes in Guadeloupe and her brother, Pierre, had gone to Haiti on an expedition. He had met Olnel, who was now owner of a chain of luxury hotels, having converted all his family's homes into hotels for American tourists and become a millionaire. To think that twenty years earlier they had set the world to rights, talked about happiness for man and liberation for women. Now they were both in countries largely destroyed by dictators, and they were compromising. Yes, compromising! What had gone wrong? What part of them had died with their youth?

It was not Delphine's suicide which had driven them apart. It was Zek, and nobody else. For him it had been the high point of his career, preaching to them both, driving home how guilty they were, repeatedly digging up this corpse which their love had laid to rest, taking the unfortunate Christophe under his wing – Christophe, whom Olnel used as a tool for blackmail, and who had been shunned once Delphine was dead.

'He'll be my son, my son. He'll take my name,' Zek insisted, a noble father. It would be unfair to criticise him on that point. Zek did consider Christophe as his own son. He used to change his nappies, cradle him and feed him, and when she returned from her crazed, fruitless wanderings through Paris, Marie-Hélène would find the baby asleep, the table laid and Zek messing with spaghetti bolognaise. That's how he had worn her down. She did not love him. She had told him over and over again. Each time he merely laughed as if he did not believe a word. He had worn her right down. One evening, when she had been more desperate and worn out than usual, she had agreed to marry him. Olnel, who had been called back to Haiti for family business, had stopped writing.

To be quite honest, the idea of going to Africa had had a lot to do with it. Returning to Guadeloupe had meant little more for Marie-Hélène than going back to her mother. The island had symbolised one thing: her mother; a womb in which she could retreat from her suffering, eyes closed, fists clenched, soothed by the throbbing blood circulating round her. But her mother was dead. The grief of having lost her for ever, of not having been near her at the last moment, had made her hate the island and it had become like a sterile womb, never to nurture a foetus again. So Africa, Mother Africa, had appealed to her imagination and raised her expectations. She had married Zek at the registry office in the 15th district of Paris almost a year after Delphine's death.

She picked up her sewing which had dropped into her lap. She had always hated needlework and was trying awkwardly to stitch the word 'Baby'. What would her mother have said if she had seen these irregular stitches, a mark of her daughter's impatience and frustration? Her own light fingers had used to nimbly decorate layettes, linen, blouses and serviettes. When she had been small, Marie-Hélène had loved going with her mother to fairs and jumble sales, organised by the sisters of Saint Joseph de Cluny, where Alix's work would fill a whole stand on its own. The ladies in silk dresses, like Alix, holding little girls in organza frocks, like herself, had cooed over the finesse and originality of the embroidery and paid a small fortune for a couple of serviettes. Next to the Italian jeweller's there had been a boutique that also sold these little works of art, and where they had stopped by twice a month to collect payment in sealed envelopes. It took years for Marie-Hélène to realise that this seemingly futile, apparently whimsical pastime had procured a relative financial independence for her proud and neglected mother. That's why she had been so keen that her daughters should study, especially the gifted elder one. That's why she used to repeat that a woman should be capable of earning her living! Like

63

her, Marie-Hélène had fallen by the wayside. Two years of economics, a brilliant future. Then, nothing.

She laid down her embroidery and got up stiffly. Leaning over the balustrade she saw Sokambi bent over her bowls of dye, beyond the hedge of poinsettias. She too, despite her age and the disappointments she had suffered in life, had set a courageous example. Marie-Hélène did not hold it against Sokambi for having urged Zek so many times to reject her. The old woman belonged to a rigid world where a fault had to be punished. Sometimes she regretted that Zek had not obeyed his mother as then she would have had to make a new life for herself. What course would she have taken? At that moment Zek's car drove up the long drive bordered with thorn bushes, whose little yellow, perfumeless flowers she had never been able to name. At the sight of her husband she had that familiar feeling of exasperation and bitterness mingled with pity and tenderness. She heard him come up the front steps, then up the inside stairs, and stop for breath on the landing. Too much drink, too many women – he was out of shape. Then he walked onto the balcony and announced hurriedly: 'I've invited Madou to dinner with us tomorrow evening.'

She stared at him, taken aback, and he quickly went on to explain: 'Dearest, I really think we should stop harking back to the past.'

'What has he promised you to make you so generous?' she asked in a derisive tone.

He laughed good-humouredly. 'You're never very magnanimous when it comes to justifying anything I do, are you?'

'Why invite him when we have so little? We've practically no glasses or decent plates, no dinner service. Do you want to make sure he sees he's done better than you have?' she went on.

Zek shrugged his shoulders. 'I haven't tried to do better. I have tried to live peacefully as an honest citizen. You should know, you can't exactly abdicate all responsibility.' In their daily bickering he had just scored a point. How unjust she could be! If he had not had to leave N'Daru because of her, perhaps he would now have been a secretary of state, a regional governor or a minister, who knows? But then he had never understood politics. What was there to understand anyway? It was simply a matter of reeling off the slogans of the Political Bureau and singing the praises of Toumany.

Marie-Hélène got up and decided to go down into the garden. She would make one or two rounds to try and encourage the baby on its way. Why didn't her labour pains start? The prospect of having dinner with Madou was a dreaded one. Instead of wishing for a reconciliation between the two brothers, she feared it. It would wipe out in one go a part of their lives in which she had played the leading role; it would mean they had reached the age of forgiveness and tolerance – in other words, old age. She would have liked to pick a quarrel with Zek but he had gone into the bedroom, humming to himself.

As she stopped at the foot of the steps, Christophe was parking his moped against the trunk of a mango tree. Seeing her, he instinctively buttoned up his blue cotton shirt which was wide open and came and took her arm. He smelt slightly of sweat. His skin felt warm through his thin cotton shirt. Marie-Hélène was all the more devoted to Christophe as she felt she had wronged him. After all, she had deprived him of a mother. 'Did you work hard today?' she asked him affectionately.

'What's it got to do with you?'

Such an uncharacteristic outburst took her by surprise. 'Aren't I entitled to ask you how your work is going? You are taking your exams in a few months time,' she protested.

He raised his eye heavenwards. 'I'll pass, I'll pass. I'm one of the top five in the class. It's not that.'

'Then what is it? Have you fallen in love?' Her voice became unintentionally ironic, as if in Rihata it would be difficult to find anything worthy of love.

Christophe sighed in exasperation and suddenly let out: 'Tell me about my mother.'

Marie-Hélène started. Her thoughts were turning more

65

and more these days to Delphine, realising that in the end she knew nothing about this sister whom she had thought she loved. Throughout their childhood, and their teens, Delphine had always trailed in her shadow. She had seemed to be proud of her older sister's beauty and intelligence which everyone boasted of, rather as they did of the family jewels or estate. Their mother used to hug her: 'Who's gorgeous too, mummy's fair little girl!' And she had smiled. What had these smiles hidden: The Des Ruisseaux used to lament over her short, curly hair.

'Fortunately, you've got a nice skin and lovely eyes,' her grandmother had sighed.

This had referred to her almost white skin and grey eyes. When they had lain under the gnarled guava tree Marie-Hélène had admired her sister's sparkling eyes which widened and narrowed successively.

'I wish I had eyes like yours.'

'You can't have everything. So there,' retorted Delphine.

And they fought together for the pleasure of feeling the warmth of their bodies.

Olnel had been the first time Delphine had acted alone. She found him all by herself and plied her sister with questions: 'What do you think of him?'

Marie-Hélène had not dared reply.

How could Delphine have possibly faced up to her failure? She had preferred to lie down and die. Could she possibly tell this story to Christophe? It might deal a fatal blow to his equilibrium and his peace of mind. He might become bitter. It might alienate him. He might hate her, and Marie-Hélène could not bear that. So out came the usual story of clichés and lies and Christophe sighed. How could he get at the truth? Who would tell him? He felt hemmed in by a wall. On the other side was adult life with all its terrible dramas. To get there he would have to jump it. Probably a jump fraught with peril. But it would be better than this false tranquillity, this childhood state in which he was being kept. He thought of Sia who was younger yet maturer than he was. What

66

about asking her to help find him the truth?

If he could have seen Sia at that precise moment, a good many illusions he had concerning her would have been dispelled. For once he would have caught her off the defensive. She had skipped her maths class and was biting her nails in a small room pretentiously called the library because a few shelves that were falling to pieces held several well-worn books.

Sia was holding a copy of *Anna Karenina* which she had already read five times. Since the family possessed so few books she was obliged to read the same ones several times over. Without being so bold as to compare her life to that of the heroines in these novels, Sia still had the impression that an immense injustice was being done her. Growing up in Rihata and living in a country like her father's! A few months ago the only cinema in Rihata had shown *Gone with the Wind*. People were still talking about it. But all Sia saw in this great epic was a world she was never to know, the world of passion, which her mother had experienced before coming to vegetate in this god-forsaken hole! She instinctively made Marie-Hélène responsible for their present condition. Whereas everybody around her was accusing the political regime, Toumany and his dictatorship, she held only her mother to blame. It was because of her and her alone that she was deprived of the joys and riches to which her youth was entitled. She suspected past mistakes, even crimes, for which they were now all paying. Especially her father. But that did not make Zek any more likeable. On the contrary. Like Sokambi, and for almost identical reasons, she would have liked to see him in control, rid of the hold of a woman who was nothing but a dead weight in his life, discipline her and put her on a straight path again. Sia would have been cruelly overjoyed at such a humiliation of her mother.

SIX

Teresa, Victor and Albert looked down the ill-defined, dusty street in front of them. A group of ragged children were dragging tin cans on the end of a string. Some young girls in faded *pagnes* were waiting for water to drip out of a tap held in place with bits of wire. Victor went up to them and asked: 'Is this where the mechanic, Masisi, lives?'

His question was met with a long silence, so long that he thought they would never answer. Then one of the girls made an indefinable gesture and murmured: 'It's up there.'

They had arrived in Bafing, a small town some fifty-five miles from Farokodoba, and Victor was pleased they had covered so much ground in spite of their hazardous means of transport. The first taxi they had taken, an open backed Toyota, had had four punctures. With the fourth, the driver and his mate had given up trying to mend the tyres and everybody had clambered into an enormous overladen truck carrying baskets of kola nuts. It had left them at a crossroads and they had had to wait hours until a taxi decided to take the same route. When, finally, one did stop and make room for them, it broke down as well, and in exasperation Victor, Teresa and Albert made the last few miles on foot to Bafing. Here Muti had given them the name of a nephew of her late husband, whom he had brought up and who occasionally took in comrades in difficulty. They recognised Masisi's house by the narrow strip of land at the front which could have served as a garden, but was littered with scrap metal. There was even the carcass of a Peugeot 404, its wheel rims gaping like punctured eyes. They went round the poky little building and found themselves in a yard cluttered with junk, pestles, mortars and cooking utensils. A woman with a baby clinging to her flabby breast and a puny, badly weaned child between her legs, came out from what must have been the kitchen and stared at them in a strangely hostile way.

Since leaving Farokodoba, Victor had been plunged in a bitter silence. Now he tried out his friendliness and charm. 'Hello, sister. We're strangers around here and we're looking for Masisi. Is he your husband?'

After hesitating for some time she nodded.

'Can we wait for him?'

She nodded again and then she ordered a small girl, who was watching the scene out of curiosity, to bring stools for the visitors, in accordance with African custom.

As the girl went past, Victor brushed her wrist – something which nobody could ever have done to her before as she seemed surprised, almost terrified.

'Bring us something to drink, little sister. We've come a long way.'

She looked enquiringly at Masisi's wife, who nodded, and ran into the house. Teresa laid down on a *pagne* on the ground. She was hungry, tired and desperately sad. But she did not dare reproach Victor. He was in a bad mood, too. What a mess they had made of things! She thought of the enthusiasm which had preceded their departure. The pride of being selected. Some of the camp members had made no secret of criticising the decision; they had no confidence in Victor, whom they said did not have enough discipline and self-control. They had been right, too. They would gloat on their return. She mechanically accepted a glass of iced water from Albert. Since they had left Farokodoba none of them had looked each other in the eye. Dusk was falling. The sun had slowly dragged itself over the thorn bushes, the region's only vegetation, and had then decided to disappear. A cool little breeze was blowing. Masisi finally appeared in the growing shadows accompanied by a small boy carrying his tools. He was a big, strong man with a sulky face, as black as his grease-smeared clothes. Before Teresa, Victor or Albert could say a word, his wife rushed out of the kitchen, where she had retreated to scold her children, and explained who the visitors were. She almost seemed to apologise for having asked them in. Masisi did not say anything, and Victor got up: 'We're friends of Muti's.'

On hearing the name, Masisi's sombre face darkened further. Then, almost reluctantly, he said: 'I'm going to wash.'

He went over to a sort of open shed which was used as a shower. What sort of a welcome was this? Teresa gave Victor an enquiring look, but he turned his head impatiently. After what seemed an interminable length of time Masisi came out of his shed dressed in a freshly-ironed *boubou* and a pair of khaki trousers. He came and sat down with them and silence fell; nobody made an effort to break it.

'It's been some time since I've been mixed up in these affairs,' Masisi let out after a while. 'I'll take you to Varandio's.'

'Who is Varandio?'

He shrugged his shoulders. 'One of the officers at the military camp.'

Victor jumped.

'An officer at the military camp. Are you crazy?'

'No, he's the only one who can help you. I'm no longer in this business, and, what's more, there's no room to sleep here.'

His wife silently laid out a mat in front of them, and put down a bowl of rice moistened with a little tomato sauce and, here and there, with some microscopic pieces of meat. Teresa understood exactly what she must be feeling. She was angry, distrustful and fearful of these foreigners who had come from God knows where, and were going to eat her meagre meal. Why didn't they get up and go? But where to? They had to spend the night somewhere. In the north you could count on

70

village hospitality. In contrast, this region seemed sinister and hostile.

Masisi helped himself from the bowl with his hand. 'So you're friends of Muti's?'

'I'm her nephew, her foster sister's son. This is my wife,' replied Victor quickly.

Masisi started at Albert. 'And what about him?'

'He's a cloth trader who's travelling with us.' Victor loved lying, making up stories and playing with words. It was not just a question of throwing people off the track and muddling them, he did it for fun. That is how he got Teresa to fall for him, by telling her a lot of stories. He made her dream of the glorious future they would have once Toumany had been overthrown. All the children would have good shoes, nice clothes, enough to eat and be lining up for school. Masisi ate voraciously, like a man who only thinks of filling his stomach, unconcerned about the taste. It was better that way since his wife was a poor cook. When he had finished he quickly washed his hands and jumped up. He seemed in a hurry to get rid of his visitors, and pointed impatiently to a bundle that Teresa had forgotten. Now that it was pitch dark Bafing seemed like one of the most desolate places on earth. Along the main street there were lights in a few shops showing pitiful displays of sardines, mackerel and tomato concentrate, amidst bottles of peanut oil and dusty packets of biscuits. A few women were selling peanuts and the light from their lamps picked out the occasional crossroads from the shadows. The military camp was a mile from the centre. Apparently Masisi was a familiar figure, as they had no difficulty getting through the two guards who stood with their machine guns at the ready. They turned left and started up a long, well-kept drive that led to the officers' housing. Varandio was walking up and down his verandah smoking a mini-Davidoff when he heard the indescribable old banger that Masisi was driving stop outside. He was feeling slightly ill as he had not had dinner yet. He had ordered his cook to prepare one of his favourite dishes, quails with raisins and couscous, and he could sense a delicious

71

feeling of hunger creeping over him. He took things in his stride, however, and welcomed his visitors with a smile.

Varandio was a regular officer who hated his job. Unfortunately, his father had died before he was born. He had been brought up by an uncle already overburdened with responsibilities, who quickly enrolled him in a school for soldiers' orphans. His first experience had been the battle fields of the Congo where he had helplessly watched the terrible, fratricidal fighting. He had an artist's temperament. He liked to think that he could have been a poet or a musician if he had been born somewhere else in other circumstances. Gradually, without really knowing how, he had slipped into the opposition. He did not do much, it was true, but his acts would have been enough to have him charged with treason. The military camp in Bafing was not merely intended for training soldiers; its eastern section housed political prisoners who were considered especially rebellious and dangerous, and were consequently singled out for special treatment. As soon as he knew their identity, Varandio would inform the families of the unfortunate victims, who had often given them up for dead, have messages sent and try to alleviate their terrible conditions. He scrutinised Victor, Albert and Teresa carefully, noting that the two men were not Ngurkas and the young women, whose beauty did not leave him indifferent, was surely a foreigner to these parts. They were an intriguing trio and must be mad to risk their lives on the roads. Masisi decided to explain things. 'Muti sent them ... They want to spend the night.'

Varandio reacted sharply. 'Muti? When did you see her? Do you know she's been arrested?'

The response was unexpected. Teresa burst into tears while the two men stared at him in amazement. Varandio handed round his box of mini-Davidoffs.

'It's now an open secret that Toumany and Lopez de Arias are preparing to let bygones be bygones. They have sent delegates for talks at Farokodoba, and Muti is reported to have been mixed up in an attack on one of the negotiators. Matters aren't very clear ... We'll know more tomorrow.'

72

Victor turned to Teresa. 'If they've arrested Muti I'll have to go back to Farokodoba.'

Varandio held out a well-manicured hand. 'Not so fast, young man. By now Muti must be in Rihata or N'Daru. This is a serious business.'

Victor got up and repeated: 'I have to go.'

Varandio gave a laugh. 'Just look at him raring to go! Let's get a good night's rest first. We'll talk about it tomorrow.' Then suddenly thinking that his quails were going to be overcooked, he clapped his hands to call the boy.

Victor was in agony. During the few days he had spent at Farokodoba he had become genuinely fond of Muti. The old woman had an unending stream of stories to tell of colonial times, the humiliations and extortions suffered under a white regime, and her husband's dealings with the colonial administration. She had no real political opinion. To talk Marxism or Socialism with her would have been a waste of time. She was simply driven by a calm conviction. The just and the good ought to be in power to dress the wounds of a people who had suffered for centuries. Africa should be in the hands of thinking Africans who would reinstate the virtues of the ancestors. To think he was the cause of her arrest! How did they trace her so quickly? What was the use of asking such a question? The important thing now was to act, and the only action possible was to retrace his steps to Farokodoba.

Madou arrived sharp at eight o'clock in the evening. Marie-Hélène had spent the whole afternoon wishing labour would start, and that she would be taken to the clinic. At least this would spare her the meeting which, as time went by, promised to be more and more unbearable. She heard the superficial gushings of the two brothers from her room, and she hated both of them. She had belonged to them, to both of them, and what had they given her? Happiness? Peace? Not for one moment. She was the only one who had been punished for the crime she had committed with Madou, if crime there had been. That was what women were for: scapegoats. Now they were forgiving and forgetting at her expense, and she could guess what they were saying: 'It wasn't my fault. I was young. She dragged me into it.'

'I know. It's not the first time she's done it.'

She put such thoughts out of her mind. She chose the perfume the children had given her for Christmas and reluctantly went down the wide stairs.

To try and make the evening more bearable she had given permission for Christophe, Sia and Alix and Adizua, her second and third daughters, to sit up at table. The childrens' delightful faces staring in curiosity at this handsome uncle of theirs did attract a fair amount of attention. Zek had also invited their neighbours and only friends, Régis Antoine and his wife Alice. In the end Régis had come without Alice, as she had to look after one of their many children. Out of the whole of Rihata Régis and Alice were the only ones to have found favour with Marie-Hélène. This couple, both chemists, had fled their native Guinea and were now living on the fringe of the local bourgeoisie into which, because of their money, they could have integrated if they had wished. They, like Marie-Hélène, were in exile from their homeland, their own people, and this no doubt brought them together. Moreover, they were Catholics. On every religious occasion, Alice showered Marie-Hélène with presents.

Régis started to attack Madou in his usual outspoken manner. 'This reconciliation that everyone's talking about between Toumany and Lopez de Arias, it's a lot of nonsense, isn't it?'

'And what gives you that idea?'

'Because it's not the first time Toumany has patched things up with his worst enemies. It usually lasts just long enough for him to extort something out of them'.

'Perhaps it's different this time.'

'And why should it be? Allow me to be extremely sceptical!'

Madou tried to change the subject, and clasped Sia's face between his hands. She shrank back visibly.

'Aren't my girls lovely! Why don't you ever come to see me

in N'Daru? Next vacation I'll send a plane to fetch you ... '

'A plane?'

The children were spellbound.

Despite the rough tableware, bought the day before from a Lebanese trader, and the plain dinner set, the food was good. When they had first come to Rihata and Marie-Hélène had still had some energy in her, she had initiated Bolanlé, the cook, into the thousand delights of cooking. Madou put down his fork and mused: 'I wonder if those of you who live up country are not happier than us in N'Daru, living in an atmosphere of corruption and intrigue?'

Marie-Hélène's look stopped him short and Régis launched into a merciless attack on the capital. The story of N'Daru was quite a spectacular one. Throughout most of the colonial period it had been just a sleepy village. The swamps and lagoons regularly decimated the white population, giving it a bad reputation. The only ones who had survived were the Lebanese, Syrian and Greek traders. Then a governor general, for some unknown reason, took a liking to this apparently soulless site and started draining it and embellishing it. Independence did the rest. Toumany wanted to be known as a builder, so he had had his statue erected in all four corners of the town, put up triumphant archways, built mosques and stadiums and constructed fabulous villas out of nothing, forgetting the hospitals and the schools. N'Daru now ranked as one of the finest cities in West Africa, even though some turned up their nose at this array of concrete and murmured, 'That's not the real Africa!'

While Bolanlé triumphantly brought in the stuffed carp and sweet potatoes Madou asked him invitingly, 'What would you say if I took you to N'Daru? You're the best cook I know.'

Flattered, Bolanlé laughed and shook his head: 'No, boss! I could never leave Madame and the children.'

Everyone approved and Marie-Hélène wondered why she felt so irritated. Even disgusted. After all, why shouldn't Zek and Madou momentarily forget their bitterness and hatred? That is how they deceived people into thinking everything was all right. They were saving face. But why worry about appearances to that extent? She sighed and Zek leant over tenderly: 'Tired?'

'Not me. Adizua, she's exhausted,' she managed to answer naturally. And paying no attention to the girl's protests, she dragged her up to her room. She had never been capable of play-acting, feigning friendship and affection. Zek was wrong to blame her for being secretive. The fact is that men and women are blind to each other. They refuse to be lucid for fear of hurting each other. Or having to make decisions. She could never be persuaded that Delphine had not known what was going on between her and Olnel. That was why she had got it into her head to have a baby. Oh, how naive! There, her imagination had started roaming again. Decisively, she undressed Adizua who continued to protest, although less and less vigorously. Then she lingered in the room, breathing in that smell of children which had accompanied her for years. They did not need her in the dining room. On the contrary, she would be a nuisance, sadly reminding them of the past they would prefer to forget. And what if she should die in labour? Come now, a women does not die after having had seven children. As her attending physician Dr Kowalsky would say: 'It'll be all right on the night.' But just for a moment she enjoyed imagining her corpse, rigid on a bed covered with a fine white sheet. That would show them! But show them what? That they had messed up her life.

When she reluctantly left the room, Régis had gone home and the children had disappeared. Only Zek and Madou were sitting on the verandah around a small coffee table. Madou got up briskly to help her sit in an armchair, which irritated her even more as it reminded her of her deformity. Zek got up in turn, saying that the coffee was cold and he was going to heat some up.

She realised he wanted to leave them alone and it made her shudder.

Madou took her hand in the shadow and softly stroked it: 'Marie-Hélène, I want to talk to you about some plans ... '

'Plans?' She said it so aggressively that he beat a retreat.

'No, no, not tonight. It's late and you're tired. Tomorrow, when I get back from Farokodoba, I'll send Inawale to fetch you.'

She opened her mouth to say 'no', but the telephone gave a piercing, incongruous ring in the night air. Christophe's voice could be heard and then his head appeared round the door: 'Uncle Madou, it's for you ... It seems to be urgent ... It's about those men who attacked your driver.'

Madou quickly went over to the phone. He recognised the police commissioner's jovial voice: 'Muti is ready to come clean, Comrade Minister. But she'll only confess to you.'

Throughout the evening Madou had forgotten his political role. Unlike Marie-Hélène, he had felt deeply happy in this unpretentious room, among these delightful children who could have been his – perhaps one of them was – next to the only woman he had ever loved. In contrast, his life seemed empty. A wife with whom he never shared anything, a son he never saw, material possessions he did not know what to do with, and authority which depended on the whim of a dictator. This telephone call brought him unpleasantly down to earth; he quickly took leave of his hosts and rejoined Inawale who was asleep, as usual, behind the steering wheel. 'To the police station, quick!'

The police station was not far from the regional secretariat and seemed to be plunged in darkness. Madou got out of the car. He had not been so close to nature, to the rawness of the night, the trees and their rustling, for years. He was frightened, as if something dangerous was lurking in the shadows close-by. In the distance the sound of a funeral choir broke the silence. The Sawales no doubt. They were the only ones still able to converse with the goddess of death. For them, Islam had only scratched the surface.

He decided to cross the courtyard, and as he turned the corner of one of the buildings he saw another building with some lights on. Dawad, Sadan, the Police Commissioner and a few other men, some dressed in khaki uniform, others in

Mao suits, were waiting for him in a dirty room cluttered with files. The Commissioner could not hide his satisfaction: 'What did I tell you, Comrade Minister? Everyone to his trade. Mine is to loosen the tongue of the most obstinate culprit.'

'Culprit! You don't know yet whether she is guilty. Where is she?'

'Comrade Minister, have you ever carried out an interrogation?'

Something in the tone of this man's voice exasperated Madou. How conceited! Did he take him for a child? Madou turned his back on him, but the Commissioner was not going to be put down and continued: 'When you feel the culprit is ready you have to gain his confidence. That's essential. You have to make him believe that he's got all your sympathy, that you understand him better than anybody. Then he'll spill out everything he's got pent up inside.'

Everyone laughed as if it were a splendid joke.

'Thank you for your advice ... Now take me to her,' Madou said coldly. One of the men in khaki broke away from the group and Madou followed him.

Muti was in a cell with a low ceiling, aggressively lit with an enormous electric light bulb. Madou lent over her and on seeing her face fell to his knees beside the wooden bed on which she lay. There was nothing left of her face but an enormous swelling in which neither eyes, nor nose nor mouth were distinguishable; it was striped in dried blood and, in other places, the open wounds were still running. Was it necessary to have hit her like this? She could have been his mother. He stammered out an apology.

'Muti; Muti.'

She made a sort of groan then her feeble voice said distinctly, 'I've asked for Madou, Malan's son. Is that you?' Madou lent nearer. 'Did you know my father, Muti?'

'My late husband, Banfo, knew him well. They were the first to fight the Whites in our country.'

'I know, I know.'

In actual fact. Madou had never heard of Banfo. Muti

continued in a slightly stronger voice: 'What would your father have said if he saw you in this government of jackals and hyenas?'

'Don't say that, Muti'.

'Don't interrupt. This reconciliation you're plotting with Lopez de Arias is going to be the cause of something terrible. Because of you lot, and you in particular, thousands of men are going to die.'

'You don't know what you're saying. We're going to force Toumany to free political prisoners.'

She interrupted him with a laugh. 'How many political prisoners are you going to free?'

The question hit home. A few years earlier Toumany had pardoned thirty men out of thousands in the camps and prisons. But Madou was bent on convincing her. 'I'll tell you something else. We're going to get Yule to come back.'

She laughed again. 'Yule? He's been in exile for ten years. He doesn't represent anything. The real opponents are elsewhere.'

'Where, Muti? Where?'

'Listen to me. I wanted to speak to you, not because I'm afraid of them, but because I heard that you, Malan's son, were here and your blood cannot lie. You'll understand what path to take.'

Tired of kneeling on the hard floor, Madou got up and drew up a stool. He wanted to think. What was the old woman on about? Was she just rambling? Forgetting his pity for her he became excited at the prospect of hearing some key piece of information.

'What do you want to tell me Muti? Your instinct was right. You can trust me.'

'As a token of his reconciliation, Lopez de Arias is bound to drop the guerrillas in the north whom he has been backing for years.'

Madou did not know what to think. Nobody had yet mentioned the guerrillas in the north. He had not really given much thought to their importance.

Muti's voice became feebler. 'He'll drop them. And thousands of men will be hunted and decimated. There will be terrible reprisals. Whole villages will be burnt.'

'What do you want me to do?'

'Listen ... '

Unable to control himself, he drew out a packet of cigarettes and said almost impatiently, 'I'm listening; but start at the very beginning.'

SEVEN

Fingers locked behind his neck, Madou stared up at the ceiling. He had slept very little and very badly. A new day was beginning and the thought of the terrible decisions he would have to make weighed on him. Why had Muti confided all this to him?

She had revealed that Toumany's opponents were going to patch up their quarrels that had long split their cause and meet in the north with the guerrilla leaders. They were going to form a national front and a shadow government which would co-ordinate the armed struggle more effectively. She had mentioned names and places. What did she expect him to do? Contact the rebels. And stop them from being crushed once they had lost Lopez de Arias' backing. Start negotiations with the most representative members of the rebels. You would think Yule's return meant nothing to her. Softened by exile and the fuss made by certain foreign powers, he would quickly be won over to Toumany's side. Madou was amazed at so much lucidity and logic in this old woman's head, but found her dangerously naive. If he dared suggest negotiating with these armed rebels he might very well find himself a petty official back in the Department of Agricultural Planning. Or else in jail! It would not be the first time such a brutal down-fall had been seen. The first thing to do was to get Muti to safety. After she had placed such confidence in him he could at least try and save her from the hands of Toumany. But how? There

81

was no question of letting her go. What would Dawad and Sadan think? How could he get out of this deadlock?

At that moment the cook knocked on the door.

'Boss, breakfast is ready … And there's a young lad wants to see you.'

A young lad? Madou slipped on a *boubou* and stepped into the next room where he came face to face with Christophe. No visit could have taken him more by surprise, nor come at a worst moment. But Madou was a born actor. He gave a large welcoming smile and grasped Christophe by the shoulders. 'What a nice surprise! Come and have breakfast with me.'

'I've already had breakfast, thanks. Did you find the men who attacked your driver?'

Madou made a face which eluded the question, and drew the boy to an abundantly-laid table. 'Don't say you don't want anything?'

Christophe gave in. He seemed sad and preoccupied, and Madou tried to forget his own problems for a moment. Like everyone else who met this gentle little boy, craving for affection, he was very fond of Christophe. It looked as though his father's desertion and his mother's death, which happened when he was only a few weeks old, had marked him for life, and that he needed smiles and tenderness to heal his wounds. Madou playfully held out a slice of bread and jam. 'Now what's the problem?'

Christophe ran his fingers through his mop of curly hair. 'I'm very worried about my future. I suppose it's normal at my age.'

'How old are you now?'

'Seventeen.'

He suddenly stared at Madou. 'You like *Maman* Lena a lot, don't you? And you get on well together?'

The question took Madou by surprise, as he was expecting something quite different. He thought Christophe probably wanted him to exempt him from doing his military service, which had become compulsory three years ago. Or else get him a scholarship abroad. He pretended to laugh. 'To tell you the truth I think I was a bit in love with her.'

Christophe brushed this aside with a forgiving gesture and went on.

'So she must have told you about when she was a student, about ... my mother ... and father.'

So that was what he was driving at.

Marie-Hélène had never confided much to Madou about her past and why she had married Zek. She had spoken, somewhat confusedly, of the suicide of her younger sister and of her responsibility in the tragedy, but as he knew how these memories tortured her he had not questioned her further. He had not been curious like some lovers who want to know everything and leave no stone unturned. On the contrary. He had no difficulty respecting that everyone's past has its murky areas and he took a certain pleasure in seeing the woman he loved appear in a slightly tragic role, steeped in drama.

He felt sorry for Christophe. 'Why not talk it over with her or your father, I mean Zek?'

There was the sound of voices on the terrace and without announcing himself the Police Commissioner walked in. Madou tried to hide his irritation. What was the wretched man doing here at such an hour? 'A cup of coffee?' he offered, fairly courteously.

'No, thank you. I'm of the old school. Never touch your white man's drinks.'

What an insolent swine!

'White man's drink? Coffee? You forget our country is one of the biggest producers in the world!' he replied icily.

The commissioner laughed and stared at Christophe, implying that he should take his leave.

'All right, but it's the Whites who brought it here. Our ancestors neither grew it nor drank it.'

Madou put an end to this futile conversation. 'I'm sure you didn't come to see me at this unholy hour to talk of the vices and virtues of coffee. What's the matter?'

The commissioner waited until Christophe had left the room, then stared at Madou straight in the eye. 'It's about Muti. What shall we do with her now that she's coughed up the information? Shall I have her transferred to N'Daru? We're not equipped here to keep prisoners of that importance.'

Of that importance?

For a second Madou was frightened. He had acted like a child. The room had no doubt been stuffed with microphones which had recorded Muti's secrets. Now they were going to be used against him.

Sadan went on unruffled: 'As Regional Commissioner, I have to send a report straight to the President. Before drafting it, I wanted your opinion.'

Madou cleared his throat. 'My opinion on what?'

'Perhaps you would like to conduct this case your way?'

'My way? What do you mean, my way?'

Madou realised he was getting into deep water, and Sadan was aware of it.

Sadan started to laugh and drew a kola nut out of his pocket. After having wiped it at length on his sleeve, he broke it and offered a piece to Madou.

'Well, I'm going to make my report. It won't be as comprehensive as yours, of course, as the old girl gave nothing away to me.'

Madou almost blurted out that Muti had given nothing away to him, either, but realised just in time that this was probably the mistake Sadan was waiting for, and he kept quiet.

Sadan got up.

'I'll have her transferred to N'Daru this very evening.'

'Do what you have to do, Comrade Commissioner.'

Throughout the morning the Commissioner's face and words haunted Madou. How much did this man know? Or how much was he guessing? What did his visit mean? Was there still a way of saving Muti? He turned these thoughts over and over again in his head, but could not find an answer.

Coming out into the yard, Varandio literally bumped into someone. He recognised Victor.

'What are you doing here?'

'I wanted to speak to you, and knowing that every good Moslem gets up at the first crow of the cock to pray ... '

Varandio took offence to the young man's slightly familiar sarcasm and replied, 'Yes, you're quite right. Now let me go and pray.'

Victor barred his way. 'Sometimes, brother, men come before God. I must speak to you.'

Varandio hesitated and then signalled to him to come inside. He did not like this tramp, this beggar, calling him brother – even though all men are equal before Allah.

'What have you got to tell me that's so important?' he asked as soon as they were in his office.

'I'm going back to Farokodoba.'

Varandio raised his eyes heavenward.

'But I've told you Muti is probably not there any more.'

'I'll know when I get there. I'll follow her to wherever she's been transferred. I can't abandon her.'

'All right, where do I come in?'

Victor laughed.

'It's between me and her. But I want you to look after my wife. She's a foreigner, as you've noticed. I don't trust Albert. I'd be afraid if they had to make the long trip back to the north together. I'm asking you to keep her here. She knows how to make herself useful.'

Varandio stared at him unbelievingly. 'You want me to keep your wife here?'

Victor nodded and his face fell. For a moment he seemed desperate. 'I'm not doing it out of my own free will. I simply don't have the choice. I have no proof that Albert won't be scared to death and go and tell the whole story to the first commissioner he comes across. And then what will happen?'

Varandio sighed. 'Can't you be a bit more explicit?' he asked in a gentler tone.

Victor shook his head. 'No, the less you know the better for all of us. Masisi must have brought us to you because you love this country, and hate the state it's in … For the sake of all that, help me!'

Varandio was not a man to close his heart and his ears to such a plea. 'How long will you be away?' he asked.

Victor indicated that he did not know.

'Do you need any money?'

Victor laughed again as if he were choking back tears. 'Don't worry about that.'

The two men looked at each other and Varandio took pity on this young face which still bore the soft outlines of childhood. 'I'll pray for you, brother.'

Victor did not say a word. He bent down, picked up his old canvas bag and stepped out into the dawn.

The camp barrier was up, and he was on the road back to Bafing. Victor had been born during the African independences and yet he had never known anything but poverty, injustice and humiliation. His native north was another land, cut off from the rest of the country. Illiteracy among the children was higher there than anywhere else. The men left their cattle and came down to the towns in the south, swelling the army of unemployed. The women became prostitutes, outlining their beautiful eyes in heavy black pencil. When he was fourteen and fed up with dying of hunger, he had joined a group who had crossed the border into one of Lopez de Arias' refugee camps. Some of the soldiers in charge of the literacy campaign had noticed his intelligence. He had got a grant. It was the only time he had been happy. Now he felt for Inawale's revolver under his tunic to reassure himself. He would not die without putting up a fight. In Bafing at the front of the bus station, which hardly deserved such a name, women were squatting beside baskets of food – mainly curdled milk, a kind of cheese mixed with dates and sour corn cakes. A few men, traders, were silently chewing kola nuts. Victor realised he was very hungry. And yet he had eaten twice. First at Masisi's, and then at Varandio's. What a contrast. It was typical of the gap that separated the classes in the country. Varandio's wife, wrapped in yards of mauve lace with her arms and fingers cased in gold, had watched them intently and then, furious at having to share her table with such intruders, had fallen into contemptuous silence. Varandio, little finger raised, had continued in a refined manner to suck at one quail bone after another.

Victor glanced around the square which was bordered with rickety old shacks and dominated by an ugly little concrete mosque. The doors of a cheap restaurant stood open. Stepping inside, he discovered a portrait of Toumany in full uniform hanging on the wall. It made him furious.

'Why have you put up a portrait of that swine? What has he ever done for you and your family?' he whispered fiercely when the owner approached him. The owner was completely taken aback, then he looked towards the door, terrified, to ensure nobody could overhear such a conversation.

Victor's anger had faded. 'Bring me some Nescafé and a little milk, if you've got some,' he sighed.

Without a word, the owner disappeared into his filthy kitchen cluttered with unlit stoves and blackened pots.

Who would finally plant the seeds of justice and happiness in this country? Victor had placed all his hopes, all his faith, in Lopez de Arias. The years he had spent with him were the only ones he liked to recall. That's where he had met Teresa. The arms and money from Lopez de Arias had kept the guerrilla movement from being decimated. And now they were being dropped, betrayed. What was the point of reconciling with Toumany? Politics were nothing but a dirty game, sacrificing friends for the sake of immediate interests. Victor wished with all his might that he could die. Die! Or else return to his mother's womb. He had not seen his mother for years. She was living with one of his brothers in N'Daru. Would she be pleased to see him again? Did she still think of him? He pictured her, bent and tiny, busy with mean, arduous tasks which had always been her lot in life. Then he thought of Teresa, whose bed he had left like a thief, and a lump came into his throat.

At that moment Teresa woke up and was not surprised to

find herself alone. Everything was happening as if her dreams were coming true. She knew that one day she would be left on her own with a handful of memories turned to ashes. What was she going to do now? Bafing was almost seven hundred miles away from Lusi, the small town in the north where she would easily find members of the network who would help her get back to camp. But how? With Albert, who blamed them for having got him into such a mess? Albert was merely one of Muti's distant relations, a bar owner with no political convictions.

EIGHT

When Victor walked into the *Nuit de Sine* everyone stopped
talking. They did not like strangers or unknown faces. And
here was one! Where did he come from with his short, flared
tunic in the northern weave, his khaki trousers which had seen
better days and the canvas bag incongruously marked
University of York? Victor, however, was not unnerved by their
hostile looks and went and perched on a stool next to the bar.
A young prostitute in a leather skirt ostentatiously turned the
other way. Victor beckoned to the barman: 'I'll have a beer,
and give the 'lady' what she wants.'

'Brother, leave me alone and don't spoil business,' the
prostitute quickly responded in a low, angry voice.

'What do you mean "spoil"? Do you know how much I've
got? Do you think all these good family men who are spending
the housekeeping money and can't afford to pay their children's
schooling can give you more than I can?'

And with that he placed a ten thousand rais note on the
counter. He had not gone into the *Nuit de Sine* with the
intention of getting himself noticed, but the effect was the
same. He was simply dead tired, and dying of hunger. He had
reached Farokodoba without too much difficulty. He had not
had to ask any questions. The whole village was abuzz with
Muti's arrest and her transfer to Rihata. The locals were split
into two camps. Most of them grieved for the old woman, and
were convinced that nobody would see her again; she would

89

swell the army of those whom the good graces of Toumany had thrown into jail, without trial, and with no hope except death. There were some inhabitants, however, who were quick to rejoice at another person's misfortunes, and Muti's quick tongue had made her enemies. Without further ado, Victor had caught a Mammy bus which had dropped him off on the outskirts of Rihata, not far from this bar that had seemed so welcoming. He drained his glass. One question was bothering him: where was he going to spend the night? He knew nobody around here. And where would he go tomorrow? How could he trace Muti? What if that incompetent Inawale had given his description to the police, and all the cops in the district were on his heels?

Impulsive by nature, and obsessed by Muti, Victor had not yet thought about himself. He was suddenly afraid, and wondered if he ought to leave the bar where all eyes were turned in his direction. But at that very moment a tall, well-built man came in, looking regal yet world-weary, proud yet strangely humble. The assembly broke into shouts and applause: 'Zek! Zek! Boss! Iziaka, son of Malan!'

Intrigued, Victor touched the girl's arm. 'Who's that?'

'The Minister's brother,' she explained, somewhat pacified by the ten thousand rais note.

'What minister?'

'The one who's here to celebrate the *coup d'état*.'

Victor could not take his eyes off the new arrival. The Minister's brother. Should he approach a man so close to those who held Muti's life in the balance? Or alternatively, should he flee?

In the meantime Zek sat down, and turning to the barman ordered: 'Drinks for everyone ... on me!'

The shouts and applause started up again and someone asked: 'What are you celebrating, boss?'

Zek smiled, and said nothing. He knew that Madou was talking to Marie-Hélène, and hoped that he would manage to convince her. Yes, Marie-Hélène would give in. The years had been twice as long for her as for anyone else. This small town with its stifling mediocrity exasperated her. He

90

remembered her sarcasm when they were students, and how she had criticised him for his ignorance in literature and classical music and for only being interested in film actors.

'What do they teach you in your country?'

He had not known what to say. He had not thought of saying that this borrowed culture she boasted about clashed somewhat with some of her theories. Yes, Madou would convince her. Since talking with his brother, Zek had gone over in his mind every town he could think of. He had even cycled across the Tien An Men square, shoulder to shoulder with Chinese people dressed in blue. Then he had returned to Mexico. The three syllables of the word fascinated him with their promise ... His eyes met Victor's burning gaze. And there was something he liked in this young man's face; a desperate determination. Where did he come from? As for Victor, he had already made up his mind. He would approach Zek. It was his only way of tracing Muti.

He had not realised that the night would be so long, that so much beer would be drunk and that so much precious time would be wasted. He watched as Zek gulped down one drink after another, and he wondered what it was gnawing away at this man. Why did he hang around with this seedy lot who were not a patch on him? Victor thought he could read in Zek's heavy features an unreciprocated kindness and a sense of introverted humanity. It must have been almost two o'clock in the morning when the owner clapped his hands. What about getting some sleep! Outside, the warm air took Victor by surprise, so used as he was to the cold blasts of the winds in the north. He followed Zek who walked off into the shadows of some tall trees which merged into the sky. Then, as Zek lifted himself heavily into his car, Victor whispered sorrowfully: 'Father, please listen. I'm desperate.'

Zek turned round. 'Am I really old enough for you to talk to me like that?'

'I'd like to be a son of yours. I envy your children.'

'All daughters; that's all I'm good for. Six up until now. In the old days, I'd have had a full store of rice!'

'Listen. I've come from Bafing. I'm going to join my brother who is a mechanic in N'Daru. Let me spend the night in your yard or your garage. I don't know a soul here and you know as well as I do they don't like people from the north.'

Zek laughed.

'Come now, you know that's not true. Toumany's got two men from the north in his Government, hasn't he?'

Then he beckoned to Victor to come and sit beside him.

When he returned home in the middle of the night Zek's love for Marie-Hélène knew no bounds. He would have liked to have surprised her; laden her with armfuls of presents which he would pile at the foot of her bed. Instead, his breath smelt of drink and he was unsteady on his feet. The old Sawale nightwatchman opened the gates and cast a suspicious glance at Victor. Zek pointed out the garage, where he never parked his car, cluttered with children's bicycles, boxes and paint pots. Victor lay down on the old boxes and the world faded away.

The household, however, was wide awake. Sia had stayed up. She had pretended to be reading *Anna Karenina*, so as not to have to reply to the chatter of her younger sister Alix. Once Alix had gone to sleep, she remained wide awake in the dark. She knew intuitively that her mother and uncle Madou had committed a carnal act. When the thought became too dreadful, she rejected it and put it to the back of her mind. But certain thoughts kept recurring. There had been unmistakable signs at dinner. She had been struck by the looks Madou had given Marie-Hélène, her obvious unease, and Zek's overplayed joviality. She felt that the epilogue to a drama was being played out. Vague images and snatches of memory surfaced from her childhood. She remembered how Madou had lived with them in N'Daru. Then they had left abruptly. And there was that quarrel between the two brothers. Whom could she ask? Sokambi? Despite her hatred for her daughter-in-law, the old woman would rather kill herself than take part in such a conversation.

Marie-Hélène was not asleep, either. She heard Zek come in and swear as he did every night when he bumped into the same piece of furniture.

He was never so completely and disgracefully drunk as to give her an excuse to despise him further. He always tottered in a semi-conscious state which enabled him to reply sweetly to her irritated questions, take her in his arms and skilfully to make love. This pleasure she could not refuse him was a torture, but it was her only refuge against extreme solitude, approaching old age and, perhaps, madness. Yet since there was no tenderness in her act it made her feel even lonelier and full of self-digust.

He stretched out beside her. 'I've seen Madou ... '

He closed her mouth with a kiss.

'Shh! We'll talk about all that tomorrow.'

At the other end of the town, in his luxury villa, Madou too was desperately trying to sleep. He had put the finishing touches to the report he was going to send Toumany and spelt out Muti's confession in detail. He knew that he was sentencing her to death. What other alternative was there in the light of the police commissioner's attitude? The old girl did not know much about politics. She imagined that a minister wielded power, that he could take initiatives and hide something from the formidable eye of the 'Supreme Helmsman', as *Falala*, the only daily newspaper, called Toumany. She was hoping to save her friends. Didn't she realise she was making him an accomplice, and that by listening to her he was risking his life? To keep such information to himself meant signing his own death warrant. But what terrified him more than Muti's fate was the unexpected twist his thoughts were taking, revealing a savagery and ambition of which he hadn't realised he was capable. Here he was disclosing to Toumany the names, plans and hideouts of the guerrilla leaders. By explaining their muddled yet despicable plans, he would be able to wipe out his worst enemies in one blow. Didn't that deserve the highest reward? Who could boast of such a feat? Nobody, nobody.

Toumany had been saying for months that he was tired of the daily exercise of power and he was planning to create the post of prime minister, an appointment he would make at his leisure like all the other government jobs. Who could be more deserving than he, Madou, who had both negotiated the reconciliation with Lopez de Arias and made it possible to dismantle the rebellion? Prime Minister, Prime Minister! He could then introduce the reforms which would gradually liberalise the regime. He, too, was tired of the doctrine of injustice, where some were growing poorer while others got outrageously richer. He was tired of repression, arbitrary imprisonment, plunder and corruption; tired of seeing his country – which he sincerely believed to be the most beautiful in the world – treated with contempt, anger and ridicule. Prime Minister, Prime Minister!

But did his ascension have to depend on the death of an old woman who had naively placed him in her trust?

Unable to stay in bed, he went out on to the verandah. He had never liked the night, when objects took on a restive life of their own, when the past became the present, when the woman you loved returned only to disappear again, and when remorse spoke loud and clear. At least in N'Daru there was no night. The neon signs, the car lights and all the din of western life had killed it. Suddenly, he longed for his mission to end so that he could take the plane home.

When he came to fetch his moped from the garage Christophe was surprised to find himself face to face with a very thin, badly-dressed young man who was sadly combing his mop of crinkly hair.

'Hello, little brother!' the man said with an engaging smile. 'Your father let me sleep in your garage. God bless him. If I'd spent the night near the market or the mosque God knows what would have happened to me.'

Christophe smiled in turn. 'Robbers, you know, only attack those whom they think better off than themselves.'

'That's what you think. Last week in Bafing, where I've

come from, a man was killed for three rais, and a group of women selling milk were manhandled for the money hidden in their *pagnes*. What is the country coming to, little brother? What is it coming to? But it can't be too bad for the likes of you. Isn't your father a minister's brother?'

Christophe's cheeks became flushed, much to the surprise of Victor, who had never seen anyone blush before, and he protested. 'Don't you talk like that. We have never received anything from my uncle and we never shall. Our family is not that sort.'

Victor got up and held out his hand in a peaceful gesture. 'Don't get angry, little brother. Tell me, do you know where your uncle, the Minister, and his delegation are staying?'

'What's that got to do with you?'

'My brother is a mechanic in N'Daru and he told me that one of his friends is in the minister's delegation. I'm in a hurry to find him as he could help me on my way. His name's Inawale ... '

Christophe looked at him in surprise. 'Inawale? He's my uncle's chauffeur.'

Victor stood stock still, his heart pounding. He was right to have followed Zek. He had already learnt who Inawale was. The Minister's chauffeur. The Minister himself. It was the minister, then, who felt offended and ridiculed by the aggression. That's why the police had gone to so much trouble. They had gone through Farokodoba with a fine tooth-comb, tried to make the inhabitants give names, terrorised the weakest and promised rewards. Poor Muti. But this was not the moment to go soft. 'Do you know where they are all staying?'

'In the party's villas. For once, those white elephants are being put to use.'

For anyone used to the landscapes of the north and those long, static sun-drenched days, there was a certain charm about Rihata. The grass grew strong and green, the earth was as red as sacrificial blood. Everywhere, trees spread their thick branches and scattered their delicately perfumed yellow petals. Victor merged with a market crowd. He ate rice fritters stuffed with meat and peppers. He rinsed his mouth out with water from a tap, and watched the ragged children run to school. Why did he like this people, his people, so much? Why did each face seem to offer a mysterious appeal? Teach them happiness, they needed to be taught happiness. They had never had it. The Whites had trampled on them. Blacks continued to do the same, and the people were too frightened to fight back. He smiled at a young girl who, suspicious, ran off to join her friends. Yes, they would have to be taught to return a smile with a smile and love with love.

As he was about to cross a street two policemen on motor cycles whistled at him and other passers-by to get back on the pavement. A procession of gleaming black Mercedes, flying the Party flag, emerged from the crossroads. Victor just had time to squeeze behind a tree and for the first time realised how reckless he was being. What would have happened if Inawale's eyes had left the road for an instant, and he had recognised him? He tried to imagine the scene. The policemen would have dismounted their iron monsters. The Mercedes would have come to a halt. They would have seized him, beaten him and carried him off covered in blood, unconscious. He shivered.

When the procession of Mercedes passed by the villa belonging to Sadan, the chief of police, he was rinsing out his mouth, on the verandah. He had just finished a hefty breakfast of fried fish and rice, doused with a hot tomato sauce which burnt the roof of his mouth. It was his favourite meal, and he was too preoccupied to cast more than a glance at the gleaming cars. Madou was mistaken in thinking that Sadan had proof against him. Sadan was only going on his intuition which told him that Muti knew a great deal, and must have confided in the Minister hoping to come to some sort of compromise. This had to be stopped at once, and he was anxious to have her transferred to N'Daru where the sinister political police, PPM, would get a confession out of her without offering anything in exchange. As the police and the army had to be involved in this type of operation on the express orders of Toumany, he had called the military camp in Bafing for an escort and armoured truck. These were quickly dispatched. Sadan thought it best to send the old woman off at night. You never could tell.

The wretched Mercedes forced Zek to brake suddenly at a crossroads and he swore out loud. It was not really because of them that he was so angry. He had drunk too much beer the night before, and he was feeling sick. But above all he had quarrelled with Marie-Hélène, something he always tried to avoid. It had been short but violent. She had flatly refused to accept Madou's propositions. Represent Toumany's regime abroad! Had he gone out of his mind? That bloodthirsty regime, condemned by every humanitarian association in the world? Her flow of offensive words, which showed she despised his new expediency even more than she did his usual passivity, had made him lose patience, for the first and perhaps the last time. Why, he asked, did she have to bring politics into it? Was she blind to the fact that she quite simply could not bear seeing her former lover make a brilliant career for himself? That he had almost attained the summit of power, and was looking down on her in pity? Because what else could she inspire at that moment except pity? He had not realised how much he had hurt her.

She did not breathe a word, the blood drained from her cheeks, the gleam in her eyes faded and it was as if she was wearing her death mask. He slipped away like a coward. How could he erase these words? What weapons could be more deadly?

The Mercedes splashed Sory who, standing at the corner of rue Patrice Lumumba and Alley 22, had not got out of the way quickly enough. This spray of muddy water on his freshly washed *boubou* was the last straw. He had had trouble holding onto the fifteen thousand rais Zek had given him. His first wife had wanted to pacify a Lebanese merchant who was threatening to seize their wretched possessions. The second had talked of reimbursing a woman from Mali who had taken pity on her and sold her cloth to dress the children. Hadn't women got any sense? What did God put in their heads in the place of a brain? A pat of shea butter that melts as they get older, as the Ngurka proverb so rightly says. As for Sory, he had made up his mind to give his baby the proper name-giving ceremony. For two reasons. Firstly, he meant to show everyone that he was not a beggar. And secondly, it was his way of telling those jackals from the regional secretariat that he was not one of them; that they could keep their salary – he was going to take up the family tradition again. He had already dealt a blow by refusing to sing on the evening of the reception in honour of the Minister. This was only the beginning. They were going to hear more of him!

The din of the Mercedes and the motor bikes did not reach Marie-Hélène. Ruminating on Zek's words, she lay in her room with the curtains drawn, in the half light which reminded her of when she had been ill as a child. September was the month of hurricanes and malaria. Her mother used to bend over her holding a thin porcelain cup and she would swallow concoctions made of all sorts of leaves picked in the hills. This would bring her out in a sweat and her mother would dab her forehead repeating, 'That's right, dear, sweat it out.'

With no one to play with, Delphine had wandered about looking glum. When her temperature had gone down Marie-Hélène would leave the room and the mahogany bed. Her mother would take her in her arms and carry her to a rocking chair on the verandah. Her tired eyes would look out across the garden to the flame trees in the distance, and the banana groves. Gourbeyre would sit like an island in a leafy, green sea. How would her own children remember her? A woman who kept her distance, was easily irritated and gave nothing of herself? Would her daughters understand how she suffered? Was it true what Zek said? Was Madou acting out of pity? She cursed her pregnancy which prevented her from knowing how much power she still had over him. As far as she was concerned she was sure she was not lying to herself. She hated this tyrannical rule and corruption. She hated and despised the ostentatious, fawning social climbers that power secreted. Although she had never managed to consider herself one of them, she felt deep compassion for the masses whose suffering was never ending and who were becoming shadows of themselves, slowly fading into nothingness. But was this enough to explain why she had refused Madou's proposition? How could she read her own heart?

Turning over carefully, she gently stroked her belly. For some days now the baby had not moved, as if it was gathering all its strength for its terrible journey. Why didn't it get it over with! She was tired of being heavy, awkward and unsteady on her feet.

In the meantime Victor was stuck in a bar. He had not dared to move since he had realised how reckless he had been to walk about openly, while Inawale had perhaps put out his description. A thousand fantastic ideas crossed his mind. Why not disguise himself as a Hausa merchant, draping his face and neck in an enormous turban? But Hausa merchants, who were only too common in the north where they only had to cross the border, were seldom seen in this region. He would only arouse further curiosity. In his confusion, he saw that once again he had given in to impulse without a set plan. He had come to Rihata to find Muti. That was all very well. But how? She ought to be in the police headquarters. What help could he be to her? There was no use his getting arrested as well.

The bar in which he had taken refuge looked a lot different from the *Nuit de Sine*. It was the haunt of noisy, chattering college students who were the only section of the population that Toumany had not succeeded in reducing into complete zombies. They still dared to criticise, go on strike, print and hand out tracts. In order to check their tempers, national service had been made compulsory, facilitating the dispatch of activists to actual concentration camps. Hoeing and digging under the sun, on a diet of boiled rice, soon brought them to their senses! There were no more grants for studying abroad, either. Abroad was a dangerous place, where they taught the detestable ideology of Marxism-Leninism and where they spoke of democracy and human rights. But above all, there were no more imports of subversive literature. All that the national bookshops had to offer was 'Toumanyism' in paperback with a special schools edition.

Victor was surrounded by much drinking and laughter. A tall boy at the end of the counter was doing an imitation which must have been a close resemblance to life, as applause broke out from all quarters. Victor weighed up his solitude. What would be the reaction of these children, who thought they were being brave, if he told them who he was? If he told them of the camp he came from? Of guerrilla warfare? At that moment a group ran in shouting. 'Quick, come and see what's going on!'

Victor rushed outside with the others.

The vehicle that was coming down the rue Patrice Lumumba was nothing particular to look at and would not have attracted attention in a sophisticated town such as N'Daru. It was a dark green Peugeot van encased in wire netting, its sides pierced with small holes. Soldiers in dark green uniforms were seated in the front, and one carelessly pointed his machine gun at passers-by. Apparently, the students were not the only ones to be intrigued by the sight, as everyone had stopped in the street and the place was abuzz with remarks. Rihata had never seen the likes of it before! First the Minister's visit, for reasons everyone now knew, and now this!

'Where are they going?'

'Perhaps to reinforce the Minister's guard? It seems he was attacked.'

'No, it was his driver.'

As the van disappeared around a bend, a young boy got off a Yamaha. He was greeted with shouts. He would know where this strange vehicle was going and why. The boy's name was Fadd, Dawad's seventeen year old son, who despite his father's job, or because of it, was a militant member of an extreme left-wing student organisation. Fadd looked around, saw nothing suspicious, but lowered his voice. 'They're transferring the people who attacked the Minister's driver to N'Daru.'

'Ah, they've found them then? How many are there? Who are they?'

Fadd indicated he did not know and dragged his friends into the bar. Victor stood stock still. Cold sweat trickled down his neck and spine. They were taking Muti to N'Daru. One more person in the swelling number of political prisoners who had never been tried and were dying from deprivation and torture in a camp. Victor recalled her face, her sharp eyes, her enormous size, her arms with their mountains of fat and her hands so skilled at trussing a chicken, chopping up cassava leaves or kneading dough. Such a beloved figure. All this was his fault. He had not been able to resist the pleasure of outsmarting Inawale. Why hadn't he followed the plan of action laid down at the camp?

'Have you found the person you're looking for?'

Victor emerged from his daze and looked up. Christophe was standing in front of him, smiling.

He tried to smile in turn. 'Not yet, but believe me, I'll find him.'

NINE

Madou got up, an indication to Dawad and Sadan that they should leave. Their presence was no longer bearable. The mixture of servility and insolence in their attitude revolted him. Their looks, their voices and their laughter belied ill will. What had to be done had been done. He had given his report in the morning to one of his assistants who had left for N'Daru by plane. By now it should be in the hands of Toumany. That evening, the old woman would be lead to her fate. Madou tried not to think of her. Even if he had wanted to, he would have been unable to save her. After all, he had every reason to be satisfied with himself. He was conducting the negotiations with great skill. The frontier would soon be opened between the two countries. The seeds of healthy co-operation would be sown. For the time being, there was only one point on which he had failed. Marie-Hélène had greeted his propositions with sarcasm and a resounding 'no'. But he would not consider himself beaten. He would not give up. And it would not be long before he would make a fresh attempt.

Once he had seen his guests out, he clapped his hands to call one of the stewards placed at his service. He would have a bath, shave and change. He had not had so much free time for ages. In N'Daru it was the infernal round of work and receptions. He made love to his wife between two and five in the morning and to his mistresses at the start of the afternoon – during those brief moments after lunch and before the inner council meetings. In Rihata, time became that lazy, languid substance which he had known as a child.

Once he had changed, he decided to go and look for Inawale who was staying with the other subordinates, drivers and bodyguards in small bungalows at the end of the grounds. Although nobody had blamed him for it, Inawale's misadventure had made him moody and taciturn. You got the impression that his pride had been dealt a severe blow. Madou put a hand on his shoulder: 'I'm going to walk to my brother's. Come and fetch me later.'

Ah, the joys of walking! Night had just fallen. The Lebanese merchants in the rue Patrice Lumumba were closing their heavy iron doors while the cigarette, match and date sellers took over the sidewalks. In front of the cinema, the women were setting up their peanut stalls and their kids were crawling in the dust. Youngsters were crowding into the one and only record shop, and you could hear the resounding voice of Bob Marley singing *The children of Jah*. Toumany had wanted to build a wall around the country to bring it to its knees in the ensuing darkness. But he could not keep out the echoes of the outside world, and Madou would be the one to bring back the light and dismantle the wall. He would do it slowly and skilfully.

Arriving at his brother's villa, he got the strange impression that Marie-Hélène had become one of the little girls running through the garden, and that she was inviting him to play. He stood still for a moment, and then went up to the youngest who was sitting on the doorstep tearing apart a toy with a child's grim determination. He lifted her up while she shouted in protest, revealing her white pointed teeth in her black gums, a sign of good luck. He had never been very interested in young children, even his son. But he liked the feeling of this little, soft struggling body which at one time had found refuge inside his mistress.

He waited for Marie-Hélène in the dilapidated sitting room, a stranger to its intimacy: a worn leather sofa lined by the feet of children, a jumble of furniture and large Bossama tapestries hung on screens – a pathetic reminder of the time when Marie-Hélène had tried to create a pleasing interior. She took so long to join him that he began to wonder whether she was refusing to see him, as if he were an unexpected suitor. When at last she appeared he realised she had gone to enormous trouble which he thought quite unnecessary. She had powdered her face, made up her eyelids and draped herself in a shawl. Educated from an early age to consider motherhood as the loveliest of feminine attributes, he had no idea that she could imagine herself at a disadvantage.

Since they had met the day before, Marie-Hélène had had time to realise the absurdity of her situation. For years she had dreamed of nothing else but leaving Rihata, and of setting off for places where life would not leave a bitter taste in her mouth. She realised she would never experience any of the great adventures she had hoped for when she was young. She was not the wife of a leader, an orator or a militant; nor was she a leader, an orator or militant herself. She had not alleviated suffering, she had not healed any wounds and she had not pushed back the borders of ignorance. She had built nothing and rebuilt nothing. But there was more to life than this torpor. If, like a child in primary school, she had been given a composition entitled 'Describe a day in your life', she would not have known what to write. Now that she had been given the opportunity to start a new life she was turning up her nose at it. Who would ask Zek, an obscure embassy secretary, to account for Toumany's crimes? Wasn't she entitled to a little comfort, failing happiness? She would meet other people again, laugh and no longer sleep away her days. Madou, who was expecting a hostile attitude, was surprised to find a person half in agreement with him. He took her arm and they went down into the garden.

Sia, sitting in front of her grandmother's house, saw them emerge from the central alley. She was holding a calabash of sour milk that her grandmother had practically ordered her to drink. Although Sokambi did not play her rightful role in her son's home, her granddaughters accorded her a special place.

They could not understand her fits of anger or indulgence since they corresponded to an unfamiliar set of traditions and her strange conception of the world. Sokambi, for instance, would go into a rage if one of them handed her something with their left hand. Or if they chased each other in the dark calling each other by name. Why?

Sia, who for years had been the most reserved and isolated of all the children, was growing closer to her grandmother. Not a day went by without their taking a meal together or Sia taking an interest in her grandmother's cloth-making. She knew that in her vague, instinctive quest for those who could hurt her mother she had found an ally in Sokambi. She watched Marie-Hélène and Madou walking hand in hand and her intuitive fears were realised. What were they plotting now? She had never considered Zek to be more than a clumsy oaf, but now she confused the pity she felt for him with affection. She would have liked to warn him of the further treachery and even greater humiliation to come. As Madou came up to her she had to get up, greet him, be kissed – which she hated – and listen to a conversation heavy with implication.

'She looks just like you.'

'I was more graceful though. Sia always looks so mournful.'

'Yes, you had, you still have, the loveliest smile in the world.'

Mournful! Who wouldn't look mournful if they had spent their youth in prison? She tried to imagine her mother at her age, and her mind conjured up a series of parties, boyfriends and petting sessions in the sand. But who could she fall in love with? The only boy to please her at all was Christophe. But she had no intention of falling in love with her cousin!

Sia was not the only one watching Marie-Hélène and Madou. Victor was observing them from behind one of the kapok trees that lined the street. He had no intention of spending another night in Zek's garage, but without really knowing why, he had found himself back near the house.

How long the days seem when you have no roof over your head! When you are frightened of being recognised, seized by the collar and arrested! At first, Victor had hung around a market, hoping to pass unnoticed among the unfortunates there who begged, slept, scratched themselves and tried to get passers-by interested in their fate. Then, on the stroke of one, he had witnessed a scene that had made him run for his life. A large, pious-looking woman had arrived flanked by two little servant girls carrying enormous basins of food. They were probably performing a sacrifice, or some act of charity prescribed by a *marabout*. No sooner had the girls set down the basins, than the rush was on. The crowd of wretches cursed and fought for a place around this unexpected banquet while the woman – full of her own importance – exhorted them to remain calm. They were like dogs. Like animals on heat. Finally, since nobody heeded her, one of the basins rolled over, spilling its precious contents. The men had then scrabbled in the sand, mixed with spittle and urine, and had managed somehow to stuff themselves full.

He had fled from their bestial faces. They had reminded him of the refugee camps in which he had spent part of his youth where, to survive, it was every man for himself at whatever price. On leaving the mosque he had taken refuge in the cemetery, watching the ash-coloured vultures half asleep on the mounds of reddish earth. At least there was nobody there. Only once did a procession come into view. A ragged procession of poorly-dressed men; they were burying a virgin. He recognised the red mat. Then what had he done? He had lost track; he had watched the sun go down and then found himself in the neighbourhood of Zek's house.

He guessed at once that the man walking in the garden was Zek's brother, the Minister. Although quite unlike his older brother, he looked like a member of the family. Whereas Zek was immediately likeable, his brother's arrogance and aloofness inspired the opposite feeling. You could sense he was a self-made man who had little time for other people's weaknesses. A man of pride, infatuated with power. A man of authority hating obstacles. And yet, his attitude to his brother's wife on his arm was deliberately and desperately humble, and somehow disturbing. For the time being, Victor had only one idea in mind. These ministers and people of their sort never travelled on foot. So where was Inawale? The old Sawale watchman arrived, wobbling on his bicycle he had bought on credit, thanks to a downpayment by Zek. Victor was reluctant to go up to the gate to get a better view. He sat down under the kapok tree, determined to spend the night there if need be. Why was he watching the Minister? Why was he hoping that Inawale would turn up at any moment? He could not say. All he knew for the time being was that his life centred around these two people.

He had been there for about three-quarters of an hour when a powerful roar came up the street. He jumped behind the tree and crouched where it was darkest. The Mercedes at last! It stopped, the driver got out and as he passed under the lamp Inawale's face could be seen clearly in the light.

Like all good flunkeys, he made sure his master saw him as he pushed open the gate, and then went and sat on the front steps. Madou did not seem in a hurry to leave, and Victor wondered how much longer he was going to pace up and down, a pregnant woman on his arm, amidst a crowd of excited children, while it grew gradually darker and the spotlight in the branches of the frangipani shone out like a lighthouse. Madou decided at last to leave, and gestured discreetly to his lackey who ran into the street to open the door of the Mercedes. He remained standing in this position quite some time while the Minister kissed his nieces and sister-in-law, and said farewell to the boys, the old watchman and the little servant girls, like a man whose duty it is to please.

He got into the car and for a brief moment Victor caught a glimpse of the face he hated. Yes, hated! When had this hatred started? He had probably always had it in him, like a sick person not knowing he has cancer. Perhaps it had started the day before, when he had heard of Muti's fate. Perhaps it was starting right at this moment. In any case, it was there, burning, depraved and famished like a wild animal. He would not rest until he had expelled it from his guts in one violent, fateful gesture that would liberate him and allow him to continue to remain alive. He stroked his gun under his tunic. He had always known there was no other way out. Madou had to be killed. The Minister had to be killed.

The soldiers manoeuvred Muti into the van They could not help showing respect for her age and sex. 'Sit down Muti. We've got two hundred and fifty miles to do!'

Muti was not afraid. She had no desire to know where they were taking her. Why all these men in arms around her? Did this mean the hour of death was approaching? So what? Isn't death the end of the journey? Muti had not always been fat, just as she had not always been old. As the fourth child of a traditional chief, she had been one of the prettiest girls of her generation. At the age of thirteen, her father had betrothed her to Banfo, from a poor family, but a student in Dakar. A few years later she had married him without ever having had the opportunity of getting to know him better. They had seen each other barely two or three times and always in the family compound surrounded by stepmothers, children, friends and neighbours. He was a tall boy, rather intimidating in his suit with a pocket watch which he constantly consulted. He used to lead his pupils to the school gate where he would clap his hands to dismiss them. What a husband he had been! He himself had taught her to read and write so that she could understand and share his books.

'One day,' he used to say, 'the Whites will be forced to leave and the country will be a carpet of flowers.'

He had died before they left, and perhaps it was better that way. How would he have reacted to the turmoil which had followed? He who had believed that it was enough, being black, to love one's fellow blacks and wish them happiness.

One of the soldiers in the front opened the sliding partition. 'Here we go, Muti.'

As the van left the police-station yard Muti pressed her face against one of the holes, but could not see much. It was very dark and must have been very late. Had she been right to have trusted Madou? She was convinced she had been. She firmly believed that the son of a just man could not betray his blood ties. Perhaps her life would be sacrificed, but at least the others would be saved.

One of the soldiers accompanying her had already fallen asleep and his gun lay on his knee like a toy grown too heavy. The others were crunching kola nuts and pushing pawns in a game she had never seen before. She felt an immense pity for them. They had not been taught to understand the world, to love their fellow men and hate exploitation, but to kill. They had been given murderous weapons and taught the gestures of death. What a waste!

The van was now travelling over a poorly-made track, filled with ruts, and Muti realised they were making a detour to avoid the tarmac road from Rihata to Bohan. Why? For a moment she was scared and then regained control of herself.

Madou, son of Malan, could not be a traitor. Everything would work out for the best.

TEN

Rihata's big market day was Saturday, the fourth day in the Ngurka week. It used to attract people from miles around, representing every ethnic group: tall Bossama warriors, recognisable by their tribal scars and wild looks, polishing their teeth as they crouched, waiting for custom; Sawales who lived along the river Salémé, carrying fresh, dried and smoked fish in oblong, coffin-like baskets; and Ngurkas, of course, for Rihata had once been part of their empire, who were farmers beyond compare, selling all the produce of the earth. Alas! Times had changed. The market was now poor and practically deserted. If you wanted to find any goods worth having, you had to get there very early and pounce on any woman who arrived with a basket on her head. No use trying to haggle. Too many buyers haggling for too little produce had spoilt the business. Sokambi managed to bring down the price of a handful of peanut paste which came from the north.

'I'm only doing it because it's you. You were a mother before I was and gave birth to a lot of sons,' came the usual remark from the woman.

Although it was clichéd it struck home. No, Sokambi had not had a lot of sons. She had only had one, Zek, who had come home late again last night. Why couldn't he stay at home and keep an eye on his wife and brother? Couldn't he see that his brother had started flirting again? Sokambi had

110

watched them walking together the day before and had not been able to sleep all night. What were they plotting? What further humiliation? At that moment someone called her and, turning round, she recognised Sory, the *griot*, followed by a small boy staggering under the weight of a sack of rice.

'Mother Sokambi, remind your Iziaka that I'm holding my son's name-giving ceremony today. My joy will not be complete if he doesn't come. You too Mother Sokambi, honour my home with your presence.'

Sokambi nodded, but it was pure form. In the old days, name-giving ceremonies were worth the trouble. The family would slaughter half a dozen sheep and each guest would leave with his share of meat wrapped in carefully-washed leaves. As for the poultry, there was just no counting. There was every drink imaginable from palm wine and the local fruit juices to the white man's strong spirits and fine wines. But nowadays there were not many who could even afford to cook a goat, and gallons of tomato concentrate were used to wet as much rice as possible.

Sokambi arrived in sight of the house. One of the boys was washing down Zek's car while Bolanlé hurried out to the market. She looked at the corner bedroom that belonged to her son and daughter-in-law. The sun would have almost reached mid-day before the latter deigned to rise. Then she would sit on the balcony and remain daydreaming, drinking black coffee and chain smoking. What an enigma of a woman! Were they all the same where she came from? Sokambi had never been able to understand where that was, even though Zek had tried to explain. Former slaves taken from Africa, who had become like the white man and now thought themselves superior to the Africans, their ancestors. What a mess!

Sokambi gave one of the small servant girls her basket and sat down on a stool while another girl quickly brought her morning rice. The day was going to be a busy one. The sellers who were arranging her *pagnes* were leaving the next day for N'Daru. A big order had to be finished and she was calculating the return when she saw Zek arrive. Already up!

111

He sat down opposite her and she thought she saw a look of hope on his face. She was respectful of his silence, however, and waited until he spoke.

'I want you to see your *marabout* ... to do a job.'

'A job?'

'Yes, I'm hoping for a complete change of circumstances. I don't want to be disappointed. Take care of matters, will you?'

Zek was a bit ashamed at having to ask his mother for something he had always laughingly considered an old-fashioned superstition. But he had become so attracted to the carrot Madou had dangled in front of him, that he could not bear to see it taken away. Before Sokambi had had time to say a word, he had got up. Zek sometimes cast his mind back to when he had been an athlete and the idol of his age group. He had earned his nickname, 'Zek the thunderbolt', playing soccer in Asin and the surrounding area. The young girls worshipped him. The boys fought to carry his boots or wash kit. He could have become another Pelé, winning fame and fortune. Whenever he started reminiscing he would get up early and go down to the Rihata social club, deserted ever since the French had left, but still offering a few facilities and a superb pool. He would return to this youthful ideal when he was feeling particularly tired of his present life and anxious for a change. The rolls of fat around his body seemed to him to symbolise his condition. He went down to the club in his car and for a good hour ran, jumped and worked out on the bars before collapsing exhausted in a deckchair.

He had just ordered a fresh lemon juice – no, no beer today – when he saw Christophe enter. Christophe came and sat down next to him. 'Why didn't you wake me up? You know I love playing sports with you,' he said reproachfully.

Zek smiled. 'I get out of breath very quickly, break out in a sweat and would prefer no one saw me.'

Christophe looked at him critically. 'Yes, you have put on weight recently.'

Christophe and Zek were very attached to each other and the former was eternally grateful to his 'father'. They were both shy and talked little, reading each other's thoughts.

'What will you have to drink?' Zek offered.

'Tell me about my father.'

The phrase took Zek by surprise and he hesitated. 'Your father? What more do you want me to tell you?'

'There are lots of things you haven't told me. For instance, did you get on with him in the beginning?'

'In the beginning?'

Zek understood Christophe's curiosity. He too had bombarded Sokambi with questions, split hairs and gone through every memory with a fine tooth comb in a painful attempt to know why his father had preferred Madou. Why wasn't he the favourite? Instead of being proud of his healthy complexion and sporting feats his father had treated him like a bumpkin who was incapable of reasoning logically. He could still remember his father's look of contempt when he had returned home from training with the sweat on his chest and shoulders. Why do these childhood wounds run so deep? Neglected by his father, neglected by Marie-Hélène, the only two people who counted in Zek's eyes.

He looked back at Christophe. What could he tell this vulnerable, trusting child? Should he tell him the truth?

From the very start he had mistrusted Olnel. He knew intuitively that this blustering playboy, boasting of New York, Montreal and Mexico City (yes, Mexico City), speaking three languages and talking only in dollars, could not have fallen in love with the tender, discreet Delphine. Somebody else had attracted him to the flat that the two sisters shared near the Parc Montsouris. He was sure of it. Then he had stopped himself thinking in this way; it was too frightening. Oh, their duplicity! They of course, had protested. 'There's no duplicity. We love each other!'

So why didn't they love each other in public? Why were they hiding? Because of Dephine. Because it seems they did not have the courage to hurt her. So Olnel made love to Delphine out of pity and to Marie-Hélène out of desire. Zek could still hear himself sneering.

When Delphine discovered she was pregnant, he was the one she had confided in. He had become a brother to her. Gentle as a dove was Delphine. He had shrugged his shoulders. Well, he'd go and talk to Olnel. It was not the first time such a job had fallen on him. Back home, his sisters and cousins had had similar misadventures and he had had to deal with young men simply ashamed and frightened of their responsibilities and not at all rebellious. The matter was settled around a calabash of palm wine, and when the child was born the joy was felt by one and all. Alas, there had been no palm wine ceremony with Olnel. He had put on airs, talked about intolerable blackmail and ended up violently with: 'I'll never marry her, never!'

Not only had he not married her, but he stopped seeing her. She had borne her pregnancy alone, in silence, until she found out the real reasons for Olnel's attitude. Unable to bear it she had laid down to die. Gentle as a dove was Delphine. Zek remembered her revolt and her pain. Should he tell such a story to this child? He worshipped Marie-Hélène. Would Christophe find the same reasons for understanding and forgiving her? Or would he take sides with his mother? Blood is thicker than water.

A waiter sauntered up with a second fresh lemon juice and they were silent for a moment. Zek had made up his mind. This past with its painful memories did not belong to him. He had merely been a witness. Marie-Hélène had played the leading role. He patted Christophe on the cheek.

'Let's go and change. Then I'll take you to a name-giving ceremony.'

After having spent the night rolled up in a ball near the mosque, Victor was washing his face at a pump when someone tapped him on the shoulder. The man was humbly dressed with a brown woollen bonnet on his head.

'It's my son's name-giving ceremony today. My joy won't be complete unless you come.'

There was nothing strange about such an invitation. On the contrary, it was customary as a token of devotion to God for

114

families to invite one or several unfortunates to a name-giving ceremony, wedding or funeral. Victor was delighted at being taken for a beggar. He had got rid of his northern dress, which was too conspicuous, and having replaced it with a faded vest, had bartered his khaki shorts for a greyish, worn-out pair of baggy trousers.

'My house is just nearby. Follow me.'

Unable to tidy up the entire Timbotimbo district, Sory's wives had done their best to clean the compound, spreading mats on the ground, borrowing chairs and laying a trestle table for the food. When Sory arrived followed by a beggar they scowled at him; there would certainly be more mouths than food to go round and this one was quite uncalled for. As usual, Victor was not perturbed. He went up to the second wife, who seemed more engaging, and with a smile said: 'Mother, what can I do to help?'

She hesitated. 'Well, you can break the ice and put it in buckets with the soda bottles.'

As he moved off the woman called after him: 'You're not from round here, are you?'

He realised his bad Ngurka had betrayed him. A dumb beggar, that's what he was supposed to be.

Despite his uncomfortable position in this town, where he did not know a soul and so drew attention to himself wherever he went, Victor was only frightened at times. He generally felt very calm, like someone who is sure he has made the right decision. Only thought of Teresa troubled him, a sweet girl with whom happiness had been short-lived. A land on which he would plant no sons. When he thought of her at Varandio's, the tears sprang to his eyes.

The tiny compound was suddenly full and the 'vultures' had arrived first. The so-called 'vultures' were descendants of Rihata's princely families who had not jumped on the bandwagon in time and were reduced to extreme poverty, since they refused, out of pride, to accept any menial jobs. As they barely had enough to eat, they could be seen at every ceremony, pouncing on any food there was and taking away the left-overs in plastic bags which they hid in the folds of their *boubous*. Although they puffed up with pride when the *griots*, with a gleam in their eye, sang the praises of their ancestors, they never reached into their pockets for any reward. Then came the men from the regional secretariat, headed by Dawad, who wanted to prove that Toumany's society was classless and that one man was as good as another. Sory's wives and daughters started bustling around with trays while the hero of the occasion whimpered in the arms of his mother's young sister. The *marabout* had just shaved his head and shouted his name to the four winds. He now belonged to the great family of mankind.

Except for the ritual greeting on passing: 'Are you in peace, brother?', nobody paid any attention to Victor.

Zek and Christophe arrived last, the former resplendent in his magnificent light blue *boubou*, luxuriously embroidered in dark blue. No sooner had they arrived than Sory, who up until then had kept his role as host and head of the family, began to give rein to his voice. When people heard Sory sing for the first time they were always spellbound and asked themselves what this man had done to merit such a gift from God. The harmony of his voice brought back to life the turbulent grandeur of the African past, its suffering, its losses and its unchanging beauty. Sory had no need for instrumental accompaniment. Sometimes he clicked his fingers to mark the rhythm, that was all. He began to sing. He sang of Malan, father of Zek, one of the first to have resisted the hard labour, porterage and harassments inflicted by the Whites. He sang of Zek, son of Malan – a rare breed among men, and becoming rarer. It was not enough to ride in a Mercedes, to have a villa with a swimming pool, wives and bank accounts. Generosity, integrity, respect for others and word of honour, these were the values the ancestors treasured and which were incarnate in Zek, son of Malan, in an age when jackals and hyenas abounded.

As Sory sang on, the audience froze and frightened eyes turned to Dawad and the other political heads. These were at a loss to know what attitude to adopt and, glass in hand, their expressions slowly changing from admiration to open-mouthed astonishment. Yet they dared not make a move, cause a row or arrest the insolent man.

It was Zek who saved the situation. As soon as Sory had stopped, he pulled out a handful of rais and, as is customary, threw them to the *griot*. Then taking off his leather bonnet he passed it round with grace and good humour.

Applause broke out and everyone got up to give their contribution. Christophe had followed Zek reluctantly since he had inherited from Marie-Hélène a profound contempt for these traditional ceremonies. He slipped into a relatively quiet corner and then recognised Victor in his beggar's outfit. He made a face. 'You didn't find Inawale, then?'

'Not yet, little brother, not yet.'

'So you can't go any further? How much does the bus cost to N'Daru?'

'Three thousand five hundred rais, little brother. But believe me it's not a question of money. I've got no identity or party card. The police never fail to get you in those cases.'

'I don't see how Inawale can help you.'

Victor disregarded the objection and pointed out Zek: 'Aren't you proud and glad to have a father like him?'

Christophe sighed. 'There's something you have to know that everyone knows around here, I've got two fathers. Zek over there, who gave me his name and brought me up, and somebody else who's a complete mystery to me. He got my mother pregnant and then disappeared. She, poor thing, died and I'm ...'

'Don't tell me you're unhappy. If you think you are then you don't know what unhappiness is.'

Christophe could have answered that the notion of unhappiness is quite relative, since one man's joy is another man's sorrow. But he had no desire to start an argument and already regretted having confided in this stranger whom he did not really like.

'And where is the mysterious stranger?' Victor continued.

'At the other end of the earth.'

This curt answer would have discouraged anyone else but Victor who went on: 'And I bet all you want to do is go and join him, and then you'll realise that your father is the one who brought you up and your real country is where we are today.'

While Christophe and Victor were talking, Dawad's anger was mounting at the other end of the compound. No, he had not come to this vagabond's to be insulted. He should have acted on his first impulse, slapped the insolent fellow and left, striking him off the regional instrumental group and naturally not paying him a cent of what he was owed.

How dare he utter such words! A song is an offence of a special kind since it becomes engraved in the memory.

> *'Ah, the new Mercedes men,*
> *With their villas and bank accounts*
> *In Switzerland.*
> *They come nowhere near*
> *What our fathers were.'*

Some people had been thrown into prison for less than that. Dawad slammed down his glass and, signalling to his acolytes, made his exit.

His departure was like a delayed time bomb which everyone thought Zek had already defused. In great disarray Sory's wives and friends reproached him for having irritated the men on whom he and his family depended. A great many of the guests, terrified at the idea of being seen with a man whom the powers to be would not fail to disgrace, quickly withdrew, while the 'vultures' took advantage of the confusion to fill their plastic bags with the left-overs of the excellent Senegalese rice prepared by Sory's first wife. In a flash the compound was three-quarters empty. Zek, who had no reason to leave, shook his head.

'Sory, Sory, didn't you go a bit too far? You know how malicious they can be. You've got children and wives.'

118

'Boss, you're forgetting that my ancestor Kamanka Kandian, who was at the court of Bilali, told the prince what no one had dared tell him to his face. That he was a pig and a tyrant. And you know the rest of the story ... '

'I know, Bilali was ashamed of his behaviour and rewarded Kamanka Kandian with a sack of cowries and two kilos of gold dust. Just between us I don't think Dawad will give you the same treatment.' At this Sory's second wife burst into tears, quickly followed by his first.

In Rihata, like in any town where events of any importance are few and far between, people tended to get worked up very quickly, to exaggerate the slightest incident and turn it into a drama or an epic. Before dusk Sory's song had been heard in every household. In some cases it had taken on a revolutionary note:

'Ah, the new Mercedes men
We'll get rid of you
Just as our fathers got rid of
The white man!'

or even bawdy:

'Ah, the new Mercedes men,
Under your boubous,
You've got no
Balls!'

or mystical or obscene.

When Zek stepped into the *Nuit de Sine* bar he was greeted like a hero. According to one version, which tended to be the most popular, he had intervened to prevent Dawad from slapping Sory, exclaiming: 'He's right! He's right! Your reign as Mercedes men will soon be over.'

As for Victor, he was not thinking of Sory. He had of course

119

admired the *griot's* song and daring words, but one song doesn't make a revolution. For that you need precise, irremediable action like a heavy bullet or the blade of a knife. The Minister had to be killed. But how? And where was the best vantage point? His gaze ran over the enclosure wall bristling with barbed wire. In front of the heavy gate two soliders stood guard, relentlessly stopping anyone who came up by car or on foot and examining their papers. With his down-and-out appearance he would have no chance of getting through. At best he would get a kick in the behind. At worst, a blow with a rifle butt. Was there a way through this wall?

He started to walk round, but after a mile he stopped in despair – it was never-ending. At the camp they had been taught that the more difficult the mission seemed, the more it needed to be tackled with calm. The word impossible was to be ruled out. There must be a way of getting inside. He sat down in the dust and placed his hands over his head. What did he do when he was a small boy and wanted to see a film or a soccer match, but did not have the money?

Trees! He had not thought of the trees. Up above the barbed wire rose some fine silk cotton and sturdy kapok trees. All he need do was climb. All right. But what did he do once he was up there? How would he get down the other side: Jump? From such a height? And break a leg or an arm? Or his neck against a stone? Victor saw himself lying on the ground in his own blood, dying a few feet away from his goal. Suddenly he sat up. A rope, that's what he needed. He would tie it to a branch from which he would let himself down, nimbly and skilfully, just like he used to do at school. Once inside he would decide what to do. He did not yet have a plan, but he would not be at a loss for ideas.

ELEVEN

The negotiations were over. Alvarez-Souza, Madou and the members of the delegation had worked hard on a draft agreement that would be submitted to both Presidents, and released to the press at a later date in the shape of a *communiqué*. During the long hours they had spent together, Alvarez-Souza and Madou had learnt to respect each other. But the aversion they had instinctively felt for each other had only grown worse. Alvarez-Souza, who had gained the confidence of Lopez de Arias and earned his stripes as minister after seven years of guerrilla warfare, was genuinely irritated by his counterpart who had never taken part in combat and had risen through favouritism. In addition, in the eyes of Alvarez-Souza, this reconciliation with Toumany smacked of compromise and he had objected to it from the outset.

The two men gave a long and apparently brotherly embrace.

'We'll see in three months' time.'

Lopez de Arias was to make an official visit in three months' time, after the release of political prisoners, the rehabilitation of Fily and the beginnings of some sort of opposition party. This last point would make Toumany hit the roof. He would have to be persuaded that this was the price to be paid for making any liberalisation credible. He would have to be persuaded to accept that the return of Yule was a worthwhile compromise. Madou recalled Muti's words: 'Yule has been in exile for ten years. He doesn't represent anyone. The real opposition is elsewhere.'

He looked at his watch: eleven o' clock. He would be back in Rihata before noon. He would finish his personal report to Toumany in the afternoon and then attend an artistic evening organised by the Party's youth section. The next day he would meet the rural action groups who reported to his ministry and in the evening, they would organise a reception in his honour.

The day after that he would take the plane back. He was genuinely sad at the thought. This visit to Rihata would perhaps mark a turning point in his career, after which he would be catapulted to the top of the honours list. But what a disappointment from a personal point of view! How different things would have been if he had not found Marie-Hélène pregnant. What would have happened? Would they have had the courage to commit adultery again? Or would the thought of Zek and the children have weakened their desire? He had been unable to assess her feelings for him and had merely sensed an exasperated inner bitterness. As if she held him responsible for everything. For her solitude, her semi-poverty, for the mediocrity and ugliness of her surroundings. They would have to see each other again. Where? How? He did not know.

At the villa a note from Zek was waiting for him. 'I have made a sacrifice. Come and share the meat with us.'

He almost laughed. A sacrifice? Had Zek started believing in such nonsense? Did he think life could be changed by a sacrifice? But he liked the idea of seeing Marie-Hélène again.

At Zek's house a few friends and neighbours were sitting around the sacrificial sheep which was turning on a spit. Sokambi was in control of operations and was ordering and arranging things in a loud voice. Since she seldom had the chance to do this at her son's she was revelling in it and the children sulkily obeyed her. Madou sat down next to a couple who were visibly paralysed by his presence. Before he arrived, everyone had been talking about the tale of Sory which had recently ended on a sad note. Shortly after the first prayer, the militia had burst in and taken him away. His wives, in tears, did not know where he was. The district of Timbotimbo was in a commotion. In the presence of Madou – a new Mercedes man if ever there was one – the conversation had dried up and only pinched, even hostile faces stared back at him. Fortunately, Zek came down the front steps apologising for having had to leave his guests a moment. Despite his normal eloquence he seemed annoyed, and taking his brother's arm he said, 'I give up understanding women. Yesterday and the day before she was all for our little project. Now she won't hear a word about it.'

Madou tried to reassure him. 'How can you expect her to be reasonable in her condition? Let her get used to the idea ... We'll talk about it with her again once everything is settled.'

Zek tried to speak in a neutral voice. 'When do you think everything will be settled?'

Madou could read his brother's thoughts and said in a serious tone, 'I told you; as soon as I get back to N'Daru I'll take care of the matter. It may depend on the embassies. But in six months you should be out of here!'

The boys were now cutting up the sheep cooked to a golden brown, and out of the stomach came a sweet smelling mince of entrails, tomatoes and spices. The youngest children ran right and left, waving their plates and calling the latecomers with their little high-pitched voices. 'Christophe, Sia, come and eat.'

Once again, Madou was fascinated by this apparent happiness, the simple joys of this simple life. In N'Daru only the extraordinary events gave pleasure. No reception was complete unless vintage champagne flowed, unless the salmon had been flown in by special plane from Norway and the *foie gras* especially prepared by French farmers. How much ground had been covered in twenty years! How quickly an African bourgeosie had sprung up that was as grasping as

Europe's although less sophisticated. Born mainly out of the new political class it had turned its back on all African traditions, except in speeches. With a sigh, Madou took a full plate from the hands of Christophe who, sitting down beside him, whispered, 'You ought to go and fetch *Maman* Lena. She refuses to come down.' Christophe's gesture took in the garden, the guests and the sheep or what was left of it. 'All that bores her.'

'And what about you?'

Madou remembered how he hated family ceremonies. Christophe made a face.

'It depends.'

At that moment he looked so charming that Madou took his hand and said affectionately, 'You should come and spend the holidays with me in N'Daru.'

'Yes. But I dream of something else.'

'Of what?'

Christophe seemed to make up his mind and stared at his uncle.

'I dream of going to Haiti.'

First of all Madou could not understand why, then he shrugged his shoulders. 'What's the point? He didn't want you when you were born. Why try and impose yourself now?'

'It's not a question of imposing myself. I just want to ask him a few questions, since nobody will give me the answers.'

'And you think he will?'

'Well, who else will?'

There was such despair in Christophe's voice that Madou felt an intense pity for him. But these were feelings he could hardly share. He had never really loved his father who, contradictorily, had worshipped his son. This despot, whom his wives and daughters had treated like a god, who had aroused fear in the villagers and respect from the colonial authorities had only tender thoughts for his son. Whenever he went back to Asin for the school holidays his father used to slaughter sheep and consult him on everything, taking his

124

schoolboy stutterings as words of wisdom. Who could explain the mysterious world of love? He stroked Christophe's light brown hair, which, although different in colour, reminded him of Marie-Hélène's, and smiled. 'Come and see me before I leave. We'll talk about it. You, your future and, who knows, your trip to Haiti.'

Christophe looked up in delight. This trip of which he had hardly dared dream looked like coming true.

The plane would fly over a mountainous land, buff-coloured and bare, splashed here and there with blood-red poinsettias which seemed to call up to him. At the airport, customs and police officers would step aside. He would break through the crowd of familiar faces of *grimauds* and *grimelles*, of *marabouts*, of jet black Haitians, staunchly rooted in the soil of this island of beauty and despair. Then his search would begin. He would take to the hills and on the verandah of a house recognise his father by a mixed feeling of love and hatred which he had never felt before for anyone...

He took Madou's hand and stammered: 'You will help me? Really?'

Madou's visit to Rihata was a trial for Dawad. As the days went by, however, he was reassured about one thing; Madou did not seem to be interested in the traffic of rice which had been draining the local markets to the benefit of a few rich people's pockets. But this mania the Minister had for interrogating him about everything, while obviously doubting his management skills, exasperated him. A mere youngster, hardly older than his eldest sons, that's what he was! And it was these lads who now formed Toumany's entourage.

Dawad could not understand why the old generation was falling into disgrace. Whenever he went to N'Daru he had to take his turn and wait for hours in the Château de Reduasi where Toumany had set up court. He looked in bewilderment at the ceremonial uniforms of the guards and officials and at the apparel of the men and women around him. He felt like a peasant in colonial times convened by the district officer; he felt ashamed of his big, bare feet, his wretched clothes and his rough, uncouth appearance. Yes, times were changing. Overtures were being made to the Communists. There were talks of liberating former opponents and bringing back traitors.

As long as he was Regional Secretary, however, he would keep law and order in Rihata and the region. He realised that Sory's song had struck a chord with a wide section of the population. All those people who smiled at him, flattered him and ensured him of their respect did not deceive him. He read the hatred and fear in their eyes. That is why he had made up his mind to punish the *griot* severely and make an example of him.

When Sadan, the Police Commissioner, walked into his office he got up briskly to welcome him and, like all good Ngurkas, gave the long salutatory greetings.

Sadan then sat down in one of the armchairs. 'When's the Minister going?'

'If only I knew. He doesn't tell me anything. The day after tomorrow I think.'

Sadan and Dawad both had the same feelings about Madou. They were both from the original team, involved from the very start, and now they were threatened. Dawad leant over towards Sadan. 'What have you done with my man?'

'Well, your militia brought him to me in a pretty poor state. They'd knocked him about quite a bit. I've put him out of harm's way for a few days.'

'Only a few days?'

Sadan sighed. 'You know Dawad, you're wasting your time with small fry, when there are some big, very big fish to be hooked.'

'What do you mean?'

'I'm leaving for N'Daru tomorrow morning.'

'For N'Daru?'

'Yes, I've got some business to settle.'

'What business?'

Sadan leant back and took on a mysterious air.

126

'Nouram will replace me while I'm gone,' was all he said.

Then he got up. Sadan was not hard up for ideas. If he managed to convey his suspicions to the political police, the sinister PPM, before Muti was interrogated, and if these proved to be justified, wouldn't he deserve some reward for his perspicacity and public concern? And if the Minister had not told the whole truth of the matter, then Sadan' s mind boggled at the consequences. In short, he had better things to do than take charge of a grouchy *griot*.

Dawad, increasingly curious, accompanied him to the stairway. The courtyard was full of the Party's youth section dressed in khaki uniforms and red neckties, preparing the evening show for the Minister, and this commotion was the last straw for Dawad. Why didn't the Minister leave? Putting on airs as if they were all bushmen. He could already hear the wry descriptions he would undoubtedly give back in the capital. What right did he have to laugh at them?

In annoyance, he was on the point of going back into his office, when Ibra loomed up in front of him.

'Comrade Secretary, you have had Sory arrested?'

Dawad shrugged his shoulders. 'I'm not the police. I'm not entitled to arrest anyone.'

'Let's not play with words. Your militia beat him up, then took him to your friend Sadan who locked him up.'

Dawad looked Ibra straight in the face. He had not forgotten his strange outburst: 'What a farce! What a masquerade!' the day the Minister arrived, and for want of time he had not yet decided what to do with him. And here he was again speaking his mind.

'Listen to me. That *griot* showed disrespect for you as well as me; and you're one of us. You were there, you heard.'

Ibra laughed. 'I'm sure he wasn't thinking of me. My Mercedes is a moped in very poor condition. What I'm saying, Comrade Secretary, is that if you continue like this you'll push us all too far. All of us.'

After this apparently incoherent tirade, he left. Had he gone mad?

Ibra had not gone mad; he was simply sickened. He had belonged to a group of youngsters who had been given scholarships by Cuba, following Toumany's talk of revolution and socialism after the *coup d'état*. He had arrived in Havana bang in the middle of a youth festival in a town festooned with flags, and alive with the shouts of enthusiasm and hope. At every crossroads Che's handsome face had cried out to win or die. In the streets the women's smiles had symbolised the glorious days of the revolution. He had a cast-iron belief in the words justice, equality and progress. But what had he seen since he had been back? One by one illusions had faded. Sory's arrest had been the last straw forcing him to break his silence; everyone knew the unfortunate *griot* had had good reason to lose patience.

Once in the courtyard, however, he regretted his outburst. He was drawing attention to himself at a time when he needed to keep in the background to try and help Sory. All around him the Party's youth section was making a racket and, like Dawad, the commotion irritated him. Were these children blind? Blind and deaf? They were content to bawl out their slogans. They were going to stage a play in six acts glorifying the events of 28 December when Toumany took power. Were they blind to the faces of their mothers and sisters growing thinner by the day? Were they deaf to their lamentations? The country was a vast suffering body which could no longer hide its sores. They were an offence to every eye. He pushed aside two boys who were carrying a puppet and went to pick up his moped. Only one man could help him protect Sory, the very one who had indirectly caused him trouble: Zek. Wasn't his brother the Minister? One word from him to his brother would be enough.

But when he got to Zek's, he almost beat a retreat as he had not been expecting to find a crowd. Had his wife given birth? Was this the name-giving ceremony? No, he would have heard about it.

In actual fact, most of the guests had gone. Only the 'vultures' remained, having been given late notice of the

128

godsend, and they were grabbing anything that was left. A child handed Ibra a half-filled plate. Zek was nowhere to be seen.

Ten years earlier, almost to the day, Toumany had snatched power from the feeble hands of Fily, who had ruled surrounded by a swarm of Western advisors. As a brigadier during the Second World War and the campaigns in Indo-China, Toumany was used to the sight of blood. He had attached little value to that of his countrymen either, and Fily's supporters had not been spared. He had not taken Fily's life on the advice of his fetish priests. The Party's youth section, therefore, had had the difficult job of turning this period of terror – which had plunged the population into mourning – into an evening's performance marking the victorious revolution and liberation. Their task had been made easier thanks to the Party's official historians, who had distorted already the truth in the primary and secondary school text books.

That night, the play's director, Karaman, had stuffed the show full of dancers on stilts, masks and animals, which brought cries of admiration from the public.

'How about that for real popular theatre! Fantastic!' Dawad enthused.

A glance from Madou made him look down and sheepishly he had one of the Bwana guides bring him another programme.

'Popular theatre,' Madou replied, 'should be based on the myths and legends which contain the fundamentals of our wisdom.' From someone else such talk would have seemed subversive, but this was the Minister himself who was talking!

'We must introduce you to the director, Comrade Minister. He studied in West Germany.'

Distractions in Rihata were too few for the Party's youth section show not to attract a crowd. The room had been democratically split in two. The first rows were reserved for the officials and important guests. The others for spectators paying three thousand rais. There was, however, a special rate for college students and school children, which explained why there were so many young people. It was stifling hot in the vast hall which had been built by the Czechs during a short honeymoon period with Toumany. Madou made his way to the VIP bar. For a so-called egalitarian society there was certainly a well-defined hierarchy! Refreshment sheds had been put up in the yard for the crowd and people were shoving and ranting and raving against the overworked and understaffed bar attendants. Madou watched the crowd from behind the glass of the air-conditioned VIP bar, divided between an illogical feeling of regret and the excitement of a glorious future. He was going back to N'Daru, and already had a plan in his head.

He would entrust his mother-in-law, Toumany's favourite niece, with the job of spreading the idea of his appointment as Prime Minister. It would need skill, since Toumany was jealous of his authority and refused to be forced into doing things. By this time he should have read the detailed report he had sent him containing all Muti's revelations. Madou knew him well enough to know that he would read it over and over again, weighing up each line and checking and cross-checking a thousand things in his head before deciding to act. When he got back Toumany would grill him over and over again to be sure he was keeping nothing to himself, watching him through his big bright eyes, half hidden by his thick eyelids.

Why did he serve such a master? He had never really asked himself very clearly. He had been induced to do it, that's all. There was a time when he had had to make a difficult choice: continue his mediocre and anonymous life or belong to the country's privileged minority. How many would have hesitated in his shoes? Of course, there were other possibilities, all cut and dried: go into exile or fight, or join the resistance in the north, for example. But who can masquerade in borrowed clothes? He was not meant for that type of life. People are born fighting. He was doing his best. How many others in his position had attempted, at the risk of incurring

130

displeasure, to influence Toumany's whims and irrationality, and to put a stop to his murderous folly? What more could you do? Muti ... Yes, he should have saved Muti. He was just about to start convincing himself that he had acted for the best, when the lights went out.

Shouts of fright emerged from the dark well of the courtyard whilst in the bar there was a cross-fire of exclamations:

'What's happened?'

'A power cut.'

'That's the first time it's happened.'

Since his hosts seemed to consider this a personal insult, or the results of deliberate sabotage, Madou reassured them with the words, 'Oh, it happens every day in N'Daru.'

The waiters hurriedly lit candles which they stuck in bottles, and their shadows flickered on the walls. Madou looked back through the glass partition. Shouts could still be heard in the yard. Probably some children taking advantage of the darkness to cause a commotion.

After a few, never-ending minutes, the lights came back on. Amidst the ensuing symphony of sighs of relief and cries of exclamation a voice announced that the show was going to carry on. The first half of the play, simply called *The Lion's Youth*, had lasted one and a half hours. How long was the second half going to last Madou wondered, thinking it would cause offence to lose patience and give the signal to leave. And then why spoil the fun? Obviously everyone around him was enjoying the show. Little concern had been given for historical truth. The cavalcade of dancers, masks and puppets had been sufficient and Karaman had won the day. Madou was approaching the officials' seats when he saw there was a large piece of paper prominently placed on each chair. Entitled *Ten Years of Toumanyism* it showed the face of the President enhanced with a pig's snout, followed by an inflammatory speech denouncing the dictatorship, its crimes and oppression. It was, of course, not the first time Madou had seen such literature; the universities and schools in N'Daru had to be closed from time to time and bundles of hurriedly printed or roneotyped tracts had to be burned. But he would never have thought that such literature would crop up in Rihata since subversion, he thought, presupposed a certain intellectual sophistication. And all he had seen during his stay were frightened or obsequious bush people, colourless individuals out to save their skins. He turned to Dawad who was sweating and looking to his aides for action. The message was understood, and they all started giving contradictory orders at the same time.

'Close the doors and search everyone who tries to leave.'

'Get outside and arrest those who have left.'

The ticket holders had not had their seats decorated in the same way and, seeing that something unusual was going on, broke through the guards and helped themselves to the wretched tracts which in no time were being passed from one person to the next.

How difficult it is to understand a crowd! Madou would have been incapable of saying whether the faces (except for the members of the regional secretariat) showed consternation or joy, disapproval or enthusiasm. What he could feel was an excitement which made nostrils flare and eyes gleam. All eyes were now resolutely turned towards the party of officials, who did not really know what attitude to adopt. It was Madou who made the first move. With a studied nonchalance he tore up his tract, lightly dusted his seat and sat down. Everyone around him followed suit and when Karaman, who had been given the alarm, poked his head through the curtain, Dawad told him roughly to get on with the job.

Although the first half of the show had been followed with religious solemnity the second started in a din. People got up and sat down, loudly commenting on events, while others opened the windows to look out into the yard and closed them before sitting down again. Outside, you could hear the boots of the militia and the police sirens, the cacophony of repression and oppression. At one moment someone came to look for Dawad. He came back a few minutes later, only to disappear again immediately, surrounded by his close assistants. Realising he was unable to fully capture his audience, Karaman shortened the show and the second half only lasted an hour.

While the secretariat's band played the national anthem there was such a din that Madou was convinced the audience was doing it on purpose. He went out to his car and bent down to talk to Inawale who, for once, was not asleep.

'You know what happened?'

Inawale nodded.

'People are bad here, Boss. We should get out.'

After all, he was only telling the truth. Out of the shapeless mass were suddenly emerging thinking people, capable of writing and printing tracts, and causing power cuts so that accomplices could quietly distribute them. Madou was not afraid for his life, although he represented the hated powers. But he felt as if he had been outlawed by the community. He would have liked to grasp an outstretched hand, stroke the breast of a loving women. But he was alone. The woman who could console him was inaccessible. All around him the night was pierced with car headlights and the militia's torches. The biggest police operation Rihata had ever known had just begun and the whole district was cordoned off.

Leaving the *Nuit de Sine* bar, Zek passed his brother's car without recognising it. He had just been through a road block and, in surprise, asked what was going on. The two young men, who knew him well, tempered their arrogant manner for a moment.

'Some tracts have been circulated that insulted the Minister.'

Zek could not help feeling secretly pleased. That would shut Madou up and take him down a peg or two. He regretted not having taken his children to the show. He would have liked to have seen the expression on the officials' faces. So the tract he had found on his desk at the bank was not an isolated event. In Rihata and throughout the country men and women were trying to discover the taste of happiness.

133

When he entered the bedroom, Marie-Hélène switched on the night lamp and looked at him bitterly.

'Why have you come home so late? You're forgetting I could give birth at any moment.'

He sat down on the bed.

'You know where to find me, Muti.'

She hated his calling her Muti, but he could not resist the pleasure of teasing her at the very moment she was asking for help. He could read her like an open book. She had sulked all day long, refusing to come down and eat the sacrificial sheep, despite Madou's presence, shutting herself up in her persistant dreams, obsessions and despair. Now she couldn't take any more. She was tired, so tired and the only being to whom she could stretch out her hand was him. He leant over her and playfully bit the base of her neck. She pushed him away irritably. 'If only you stank less of beer.'

He bit her lightly again and this time she did not object. This pattern mirrored their relationship. At first she would refuse, and he would insist; then she would give in, sometimes with passion. 'I don't love you, I don't love you! What do you care if I don't love you?'

At the height of their lovemaking, when she was defenceless beneath him, he would interrogate her.

'You don't love me? You still don't love me?'

She shook her head and off they would go again. This phrase, which had hurt him so much, had gradually become the key to a game. Did Marie-Hélène still not love him after seventeen years? Hadn't she begun to love him without realising it? What was the good of torturing himself? He was all she had left. He stretched out his body against hers, clutching her womb. Perhaps she would be disturbed by one of her nightmares. He would clasp her tighter and reassure her like a child. To himself he mouthed those words he never dared say out loud, as he thought them unworthy of a man. Yet surely she was the guilty party? 'My love, we've been together for so many years and our paths have never crossed. You are locked in your remorse and your dreams; I in my awkwardness and my egotism. When will it stop?'

Christophe was finishing a drink at the *Calao* when he heard
the noise of the police sirens and the militia's cars. He had let
himself be talked into coming by Fadd, Dawad's son and his
best friend. His friendship with Fadd raised a good deal of
criticism, sarcasm and disapproval from Marie-Hélène and
even Zek. But Christophe took no notice of these antiquated
theories which make children responsible for the sins of their
fathers. Dawad was no doubt a swine. Fadd was quite
different. Christophe listened.

'What's going on now?'

Fadd, who was feeling slightly tipsy, shrugged his shoulders.

'Nothing that won't stop us from finishing our whiskies.
What do you think of the little Sawale over there in the blue
boubou?'

Christophe was not interested. Since his last conversation
with his uncle his one dream was Haiti. The school library,
however, had only two books on the subject. No one had
bothered to slit open the pages of the first one, *Voodoo in Haiti*
and Christophe, who despised all religions, was not interested
in it anyway. The other, a book by two journalists, was high on
cheap sensations and local colour. In one sweep, Christophe
had been initiated into the crimes of Papa Doc, alias Baron
Samedi, the extortions of the Tontons Macoutes and the
excesses of the Fillettes Laleau. He was overwhelmed. His
adolescent mind was close to concluding that the black
peoples were condemned to a sombre fate, to suffer and never
know the taste of happiness. Why was there this worldwide
display of oppression?

He sighed and once again tried to picture his father.
Handsome. Such a charmer could only be handsome. The
corpulence that comes with age and a life of semi-idleness.
Dressed in the white drill that is worn in the Tropics. Owner of
a chain of hotels and a millionaire: not very inspiring! He
would have preferred a father who was a political opponent,

135

an exile, a martyr, dead! Oh, if only children were allowed to choose their parents!

The noise of the police cars and the militia became deafening, drowning the unprofessional sounds of the *African OK Jazz Band* which was imitating airs from Zaire. Some of the young clients rushed to the door. Fadd held back Christophe, who wanted to follow suit.

Crouching in the shadow of one of the park's mango trees, Victor watched as the delegation's cars entered, headed by the one driven by Inawale. They stopped where the roads intersected at each of the four corners of the small esplanade laid out between the flower beds and the ornamental shrubs. Victor now knew the terrain by heart. In the centre was the Minister's villa called the VIP suite. Adjacent to it were two smaller villas, almost as luxurious, and behind, a row of inconspicuous bungalows for the staff. Madou got out of his car, climbed the steps under the lamps and crossed the verandah to the door of the villa. And all this time he was alone, fantastically alone, the perfect target, a defenceless victim. But this was not the place he would have to be shot!

Although it was difficult to penetrate the compound, once you were inside it you could come and go as you pleased. The regional secretariat had hastily recruited a swarm of domestics, laundrymen, cooks, sweepers, gardeners and odd job men who buzzed around chaotically going in and out of villas, washing laundry in the yard, ironing in the shade of the trees, and heating the irons on charcoal stoves, fanned by girls who also had to grind the cassava or clean the rice in large sieves.

Victor could have mixed in with the crowd, but he was afraid his northern accent would attract attention again and he hid under the tall trees, watching every movement. Unlike his companions, the Minister did not seem to go in for women. Not one could be seen slipping in during the afternoon siesta or as dusk fell. He received a lot of people, but always in the call of duty, and did not have a court of parasites and sycophants permanently installed on the verandah. Out of the dozen rooms in his possession he only occupied three; the others remained closed. The one where he worked and where he could be caught unawares formed an angle where the light burnt late into the night.

Victor had devised a plan. Getting into the villa was child's play. Once he was there he would hide in one of the unoccupied rooms. When the stewards had returned to their quarters he would slip into the office and wait for the Minister who was bound to come in and work. As soon as he appeared he would fire, emptying his gun so as to be sure not to miss him, and then escape. From then on it was not very clear. He did not see how he could get out of the grounds. It all depended on how soon the alarm was given. Would they hear the shots? Would they come running immediately? And who? The stewards were easily scared. The other officials from the neighbouring villas? There were no guards in the compound. Those at the entrance next to the gates were too far away.

Victor could hear his heart beating. Yes, now he was afraid. This time the next day perhaps he would be dead. A sheet gently draped over his eyes. Men would come and give speeches while the women lamented and wept. With eyelids closed he would hear all that and say to himself, 'The poor wretches, they've no idea! I'm at peace! No more fantasies and impossible dreams. I have come to know that the world will never be as lovely and sweet smelling as a garden of orange trees.'

He was frightened, but determined. He stroked the gun he had stolen from Inawale, quite unlike the ones he had trained with at the camp. So what! Death would come out of the barrel just the same.

TWELVE

Dawad started at the three young men they had just brought in. He already knew one of them, Falade, a primary-school teacher from the Timotimbo district. Last year Falade had led a delegation of pupils to the regional secretariat to demand more school materials. It was obvious he had primed the children to say that natural science and maths books woud be more useful than copies of *Toumanyism*. Dawad had felt like throwing him in prison, but his assistants had dissuaded him as anything that touched on school children or college students was full of potential danger. These beastly children were always ready to take the bit between their teeth, demonstrate in the streets and go on strike. And who could punish or maltreat a child? So Dawad had let him go, promising himself he would get back at him. The moment had now come. Neighbours were claiming that Falade had held meetings late into the night with other vagabonds of his sort, and that he had hidden a bundle behind his wives' mortars and pestles. The other two men were a nurse from the children's hospital and an assistant from the national pharmacy. Both were accused of having said in a bar, 'The President's a pig!', 'All he needs is a snout!'

From these outbursts to the writing of tracts was just one small step. All three had attended the show by the Party's youth section and had been unable to produce their Party card when summoned by the militia, because they simply did not have one! Didn't they know that every citizen over the age of twenty-one had to be a Party member? Now they were in for it! Nouram, assistant to Sadan the head of police, entered the office looking important. 'Brother, I'm replacing ... '

'I know, I know,' Dawad interrupted him. He did not like the young man. 'Take them away and have them make a statement.'

'I've got nothing to say,' Falade interrupted. 'Your accusations are worthless.'

Nouram looked him over. 'That's for us to decide.'

Then he opened the door and four policemen entered and slipped handcuffs on all three. Dawad liked to see things done quickly and efficiently. They had found the culprits in a few hours. At long last! When the Minister questioned him he would be able to show him how efficient these bushmen really were. He went out on to the balcony to watch Nouram take them away, and once again bumped into Ibra leaning over the balustrade watching the little group being led off. Ibra turned and in the eyes of his young assistant Dawad read so much hatred and anger, that he decided to write a report, right away to the national secretariat. He endeavoured, however, to keep calm. As Nouram waved goodbye a thought occurred to him and he shouted after him. 'Put a few guards around the Minister's villa. You never know!'

The other nodded and jumped nimbly into his jeep.

The day was calm and beautiful. It was the middle of the dry season; the sun was high in the sky and the smell of the river banks and rice fields rose up in the clear air. The sky was the colour of an overwashed indigo *pagne*. It was the time of long siestas and late meals in the family compounds when dusk was slow to fall. Dawad would have liked to have gone home, and he cursed Madou, whose visit was causing him so much work. Fortunately, Madou was leaving Rihata the next day: a special plane was coming from N'Daru to pick him up.

In the meantime, three men were heading for their fate. Falade and his two companions who had been arrested after the show had spent the night at the District Four police

139

station. In the morning the police had read out an exaggerated charge and then brought them before Dawad. Now they were being taken to the main police station.

Nouram, Sadan's replacement, was a promising young man. At twenty-four, he was already Assistant Regional Police Commissioner, and he had no intention of stopping there. Connected through his wife to the Minister for the Interior, who had been responsible for his quick promotion, his one dream was to live in N'Daru. What a metropolis that little town had become! Every time he paid a visit, Nouram was stunned by the number of high-rise buildings, the luxuriousness of the night clubs, where you rubbed shoulders with the most beautiful women, and the stream of cars. Sadan was usually jealous of his authority and his absence provided Nouram with an opportunity to prove himself. If he pulled this case off in three months, he would be the head of police in N'Daru. He jumped out of his jeep. Young and handsome, he liked to keep up a sporty appearance. 'Lock up this scum … I'm going for lunch. I'll hear what they have to say when I get back,' he shouted.

As there was only one cell reserved for political prisoners, out of the two in the main police station, Sory, the *griot*, had three additional companions. He was finishing a dismal meal of damp rice flour that he was trying to swallow so as not to collapse with hunger.

'Falade, what are you doing here?' he exclaimed.

He had been locked up for forty-eight hours and knew nothing of what was going on in town. The others told him.

The secretary closed the letter file, chewed on her tooth stick for a moment and then stated, 'I won't be coming in this afternoon, Boss, my aunt's dead.'

Zek raised his eyes upwards.

'At the rate you're killing them off, Lamia, you soon won't have any family left.'

The girl did not answer and went on chewing aggresively. In actual fact, she resented him. She was new to the department and he had pursued her unremittingly. But no sooner had he slept with her four or five times than he had become distant and indifferent as if nothing had happened, as if she had dreamed up those weekend afternoons in her two rooms next to the mosque. She had confided her bitterness to two colleagues who told her he was like that because he was terribly afraid of his wife, a half-caste, a foreigner.

'He probably preferred to pull out because he thought you were getting involved.'

Zek paid scant attention to what his secretary thought and the explanations she gave concerning his behaviour. He could not help seducing all the women he knew and had very few refusals. His desire quickly tired once the excitement of their resistance and coyness faded. Except for Marie-Hélène, he had never desired a woman for more than three months. As it was one o'clock in the afternoon he offered to drop her off at her house. She shook her head. She could not bear the idea of his being on her doorstep and not even trying to cross it.

When he was leaving home that morning Marie-Hélène had complained of all sorts of pains and he had vaguely expected a telephone call telling him to drive her to hospital. He had better go home for lunch. And yet he had promised Ibra to speak to Madou about Sory. The *griot* had not been home for three days and was being held at the main police station. What fate was in store for him?

He got up, straightened out his *boubou* and headed for the office door. Should he talk to Madou about Sory and ask him to intervene? He should not ask for too many things at once; the benefactor might get tired. And after the incidents of the day before, would Madou be in a generous mood? He might talk of setting an example.

A woman was sitting on the pavement with her triplets beside her and Zek absent-mindedly threw her a rais. No, he would not mention Sory straightaway. He would say he had come to have the latest news. Had they found the people who had disrupted the show? Were there any developments? He was not being hypocritical. Simply artful. Yet Zek was ashamed of himself. He hated injustice and would have liked to come to terms with Dawad, or failing that, have a frank, direct talk with Madou.

A police van that had overtaken him on the left and almost caused a terrible accident preceded him to the Party villas. As he got out of his car, four men armed with machine guns took up positions around Madou's residence. What was going on now? Zek had always believed that if the art of killing was really necessary, it should go hand in hand with the faculty to think. Nothing revolted him more than the sight of these weapons in the hands of semi-obtuse brutes for whom pressing the trigger was just a game. Carefully avoiding looking at the policemen, he climbed the steps. In the main living room Madou was surrounded by a dozen men who were obviously intimidated and awkward, not knowing what to do with their calloused feet, their cracked hands and uncouth appearances. The leaders of the rural community action group had come to discuss their problems. Madou was giving them a short speech on the importance the Government, and the Minister in particular, attached to the credit funds being set up for them and the equipment being ordered. After each sentence they nodded. Were they dupes? For years the situation of the rural communities had been getting worse. Whole villages had been abandoned, leaving only the women and old people behind. In the east cases of famine had been reported and terrified refugees streaming towards N'Daru had told how men were eating men for want of other meat. Did Madou believe a word of what he was saying? He leant forward, gesticulating with his delicate hands, and sometimes his lips parted in a supercilious yet charming smile. Once again Zek hated him. Not because of what had happened between them in the past. Zek told himself that, after all, if he had managed to give Marie-Hélène a little happiness, so much the better. It was because of what Madou had become – an opportunist and a schemer. Because he was young and good-looking, he was deceptive.

'He's better than the others!' they would say. 'He can't be as corrupt.'

'Oh no? He was just like the rest.' Madou graciously dismissed everybody and the assembly rose.

'Why these guards around your villa?' Zek asked in surprise once Madou had seen his guests out. 'Because of yesterday?'

'Dawad's overdoing it. He called to say he was having me protected.'

'Perhaps he's right, after all.'

Madou shrugged his shoulders. 'I'm leaving tomorrow,' he said. 'If you don't mind, I'll pass by your house to say goodbye to Marie-Hélène and mother.'

He was leaving! Would he still remember them once he was back in N'Daru? After all, he had lived for years without apparently thinking of Marie-Hélène. He seemed to read Zek's thoughts.

'As soon as I arrive I'll get in touch with Ali, the Minister for Foreign Affairs. We graduated together. Then I'll talk to the President. You can't do anything without him.'

Was he being sincere? Weren't these hollow words like the ones he had used to allay the fears of the rural community action groups? Zek was afraid for the hopes that had been roused in him.

Three boys brought in the meal on heavy copper trays. Zek could not help noticing the elegance of the china and the sparkle of the cutlery. Why such luxury and ostentation? The Whites themselves in colonial times had not lived this way. He remembered the Asin district officer covered in freckles, forever sweating, wearing baggy shorts and thick socks, rolled at the knees. Behind his back everyone called him 'soft prick' as they said he could not get a hard-on. And yet there was always a girl in his bed.

'Will you have lunch with me? I hate eating alone.'

Zek was no dupe. The invitation was merely for appearance's sake. In fact, his brother was showing him the door. He took his leave. At the foot of the steps the policemen stood to attention, not knowing quite who he was.

When he got home, the children told him breathlessly that Marie-Hélène had gone into labour and Régis Antoine had driven her to hospital.

Nobody witnesses his own birth. Nobody remembers the terror of coming into the world, whether the midwife's hands are rough or smooth or how his mother first looked at him. Probably to fill this vacuum Marie-Hélène's mother had often told her of her birth and Marie-Hélène could hear her voice now: 'You were lovely from the very start. A darling baby with bright eyes and long, smooth, black hair. Like a little coolie. "It won't stay like that, you'll see," they had said. It didn't. It simply started to curl.'

At other times she had said, 'I wanted a boy, you know; you always want a boy the first time. But when I saw you with that look in your eye I wouldn't have changed you for all the boys in the world.'

She opened her eyes and the midwife smiled. 'It'll be all right. Besides, you're used to it.'

Used to it? Do you ever get used to it? It's like an actor who goes on stage every evening and still has stage fright. He knows every line, every movement. He knows when he has to make his voice carry and when he has to whisper. And yet he has stage fright. You cannot get used to it. Each time, the drama is relived as intensively as the first time. When she was twelve she dreamt of being an actress. She had appeared in a one-act play staged by the school and had been an enormous success. 'What a lovely little girl you have!' people would compliment her mother. 'Oh, you've got two! One dark, one fair, how nice!'

She dreamt of being an actress. So she wrote a collection of plays for two characters; she was the heroine of course, and Delphine, her little, high yellow sister, obediently carried the train. Sometimes their mother would hide and watch them and could not wait until the pumpkin had turned into a coach to appear and shower them with kisses.

Someone was bending over her. 'Your waters have already broken. It will be over very quickly.'

Very quickly? And yet the great symphony of pain had not yet assembled its bass and treble tones in this little white room where she remained lucid yet distant, as if divorced from

144

herself, torn between an active and a passive role. And what was the little stranger thinking? She would soon see its face.

She was ten when her brother had been born and it had come as a surprise. For years her parents had no longer seemed to live together, hardly speaking, only seeing each other at meal times, their father always in a hurry, bullying the domestics in creole and causing her mother to purse her lips, and already peeling his fruit when they had only just begun eating. Suddenly her mother's belly begun to swell obscenely in her pleated dresses under lace and hem-stitched yokes. She knew it would have been impossible without some prior, mysterious manoeuvering by her father, and she would have liked to ask questions. Her mother had not had time for her and used to receive her friends on the verandah – living as they did in a old house *entre cour et jardin* that had belonged to the Des Ruisseaux. 'This time I'd like it to be a boy,' she had sighed.

Her wish had been granted. One morning when they entered her room they discovered a little, unknown, yet familiar figure in a ribboned cradle, dressed in a blue top three times too big, stitched with the words *Bébé*.

Pierre had escaped the constant remarks on the colour of his skin and the nature of his hair, the shape of his nose and the thickness of his lips. He was a boy, that was all that mattered. Nobody seemed to mind that he had come out a copper-red colour. In fact he had done so little to 'raise the colour' of the family that people wondered whether he really was the son of his lovely mulatto mother.

'He's the spitting image of Siméon,' she would sigh in a strangely affectionate voice.

And Siméon would take his little boy to the soccer matches which, together with women, were his favourite past-time. A sporty type, Siméon Montlouis, like Zek.

It was starting to hurt, really hurt. And yet she knew it was only the overture. The orchestra was tuning up; the bass could still be distinguished from the treble and had not combined in a rousing crescendo that would leave her panting and confused while she waited for the moment when, on a flatter note, the sound would fade away into silence. She did not remember Delphine's birth as she had only been two years old. It had therefore become a kind of mythical account, prone to all types of distortion.

'When I saw she was as light-skinned as that, almost white with grey eyes, I said to myself, she'll be as fair as day. She never cried. She drained every drop from her bottles. That time I did not have any milk, unfortunately.'

Marie-Hélène sighed. She guessed that the milk had mysteriously dried up because of her father's behaviour. Had he started having mistresses? Dashing young negresses who had cast aspersions on his legitimate wife?

However long she lived she would never forget the birth of Christophe in that clinic in the 15th district of Paris where all the nurses had thought Zek the fortunate father and had congratulated him.

Delphine had kept her eyes tightly shut. She had never once looked at her child, she had refused him her breast, swollen with milk, as if Olnel's rejection meant she had to do the same; as if Christophe had to be rejected by father and mother alike, although she had borne him only to keep Olnel.

'Look at him. Look how lovely he is,' Zek had pleaded with her. 'A baby, Delphine, is the blessing of the gods. Nothing is more precious. As my mother would say, you can't buy it at the market, not even with two hundred sacks of cowries.'

Then he would take the baby in his arms.

'No, no,' the nurses had scolded. 'You must leave him in his cot. You'll give him bad habits.'

Is love a bad habit?

Where was Zek? Why wasn't he here? The maternity wards were full of fathers who wanted to share everything with their wives, who wanted to compensate for not being able to bear a child, to feel it move and then part with it in a terrible epilogue. Where was he?

'Your husband? We advised him to go and have a drink and

146

come back in an hour or two. He was shaking as if it was the first time!'

The first time it had been Sia!

She had never talked to her daughter about her birth. They never talked about anything like that. Judged by the number of words exchanged they communicated little. Unless you counted looks, facial expressions and gestures. She knew what Sia was thinking, and knew exactly when she was calling for help. But how can you help when you yourself are drifting without a bearing? When your own life is on the verge of madness. Where was Zek? When all was said and done, he was all she had. Yes, she could have told Sia all about it in a short, pious speech like her mother used to give her while she sucked her thumb, trying to recall the big shuttered bedroom in the half-light, the bustle of the midwife and servants, and the doctor, who was the last to arrive, just in time to take the baby in his arms and declare: 'It's a girl, a beautiful, bouncing girl!'

No, she was not one for pious, edifying little speeches. So she had preferred to remain silent since she could not tell the truth. 'I carried you in anger, my dear. I held it against you for not being the child of the man I loved, the man I could not get over having lost. For being Zek's daughter. I never thought of you with affection and when finally we parted I felt so glad to be delivered. I expelled you almost in hate.'

No you can't say that sort of thing. But it hadn't stopped there. 'Once they put you in my arms, to my amazement I took to you. I could not get over the fact that I had created a miracle of beauty: almond eyes, delicate brows, that mouth ... only your flat nose reminded me of Siméon's, my father's. I watched you sleep, yawn and wake up. Sia, my first born!'

Right now she was in pain. She must not shout. Above all, she must not shout. The women who were giving birth in the general ward behind the screen were suffering in silence, their eyes closed, their lips tight, sometimes uttering a groan. No shouting. Grip the bedposts. Push. The midwife dabbed her

147

face with water which had a relieving effect and she got her breath back. No, you never get used to it. Where was Zek? She could not think of anybody. Neither her mother. Nor Delphine. Nor Sia. Nobody had given birth before her. Nobody had suffered like this.

Madou bumped into Sia standing by the gate. She stiffened when he kissed her. '*Maman*'s gone to hospital,' she announced.

And as if that were not enough, 'She's having a baby,' she explained.

He was struck by her hostile expression. What did she have against him?

'There's nothing to be afraid of. She's used to it,' she went on, doggedly.

Used to it? Do you ever get used to it?

How he would have liked to be the baby's father! The gods had refused him the anxious joy of awaiting the baby of a beloved wife. While he was standing next to this half-rusty gate, next to this girl whose antagonistic attitude hurt him, Marie-Hélène was far away, locked in suffering which he had not caused and in which he had no part. Like every man who feels a certain contempt for women, he felt a great deal of pity for the suffering inherent in their condition. It seemed to him an undeserved punishment for the faults they had not committed, limited as they already were in their possibilities and achievements. He never thought for one moment that such suffering could give depth to woman's destiny and actually enhance it.

He thought of his mother who had often spoken to him of his birth. Before him, she had given birth to a number of girls and lost several boys. They thought there was a spell on her. Perhaps a revenge by her co-wives. When she became pregnant again, she had gone north to visit a holy man who was renowned throughout the country. He was said to be versed in the science of the Arabs, and he himself looked like an Arab with his fine features and long, pale blue caftan. He had gently massaged her growing belly, drawn letters on her navel, murmuring, 'Your son will live this time,' and given her some verses from the Koran. Madou, who knew how little should be placed on this sort of tale, nevertheless drew a certain pleasure from believing that his destiny had been special from the very start.

He followed Sia into the garden. Prime Minister! As the hour of departure approached he felt a growing feeling of power. Regrets at leaving Rihata were fading. His heart filled with a joyful impatience. Once in N'Daru he would have himself driven to the President's. Toumany loved these demonstrations of intense activity. He would no doubt have read the reports, especially the one containing Muti's revelations, and they would talk about it. Madou would request leniency for the old woman, invoking her age and her husband's past.

'Would you like something to drink?' Sia asked him with brusque politeness.

He shook his head, decided to turn on the charm, and took her hand. 'Why don't you come and spend your holidays in N'Daru? We have everything a young girl of your age likes, even a skating rink.'

Sia stared at him in contempt. A skating rink! What next? Did he take her for one of those irresponsible scatterbrains who only dream of European pleasures? And yet the idea of going to N'Daru attracted her. The holidays were always difficult times, never-ending days that somehow had to be filled. Sometimes Zek took them to the pool. The little ones loved it. He taught them how to swim and drive. But her father's naked body and his vanquishing looks made her sick. She preferred to stay indoors with a book that she knew by heart.

The long holidays were the worst. It would pour with rain and the sky would merge with the earth and the river over-flowing its banks. Marie-Hélène hated the rainy season and she contaminated the whole household with her bad temper. She would be seen shivering, wrapped in shawls, staring untiringly at the rain which made ruts in the garden and slowly rotted the wood, the furniture, the upholstery

149

and the tapestries; and even the childrens' skin puffed up with mushrooms. As she dabbed them furiously with iodine, both the younger and the elder daughters felt how incongruous their mother was in this country she had never accepted. Since she seldom spoke of her own country, and when she did it was always in negative terms, they unsuccessfully tried to build an environment where she felt at home, happy, elated and talkative rather than silent and irritated with sudden fits of tenderness.

At this very moment Sia realised how much she loved her mother, how the hate she apparently felt was an artificial glaze which masked her true feelings. She loved her without knowing her, without understanding her and perhaps because she introduced into their lives all the anguish of the outside world. She tried to imagine her at the hospital, but could not as her information on childbirth was incomplete and terrifying. Blood. Shouts. Suffering. The foetus driven from its haven and never getting over it. Some people claim that the whole of life is spent hankering after this period of warmth and peace, and that happiness is only found when you finally regain it. Sia did not believe a word. At her age she imagined happiness as plunging into a whirlpool, letting herself go completely. Letting the water rush over her from all directions, in a rough sea. Perhaps N'Daru would be a foretaste of this turbulence? She looked at Madou hopefully.

'In a month and a half it's half-term.'

'OK for half-term,' he said, nodding graciously, 'I'll send an invitation to your parents before leaving. My wife has plenty of younger brothers and sisters who will show you around. You'll like it.'

At the same time, Madou blamed himself for describing this place of debauchery, intrigue, inequality, meanness and degradation as a paradise. But he realised that young people needed action and it was not fair to keep Sia in Rihata. A group of bats flew out of the cotton tree. Night had fallen and they had not noticed. Madou envisaged the long hours in front of him with nothing to do. No longer anonymous, he had lost the possibility of pushing open a bar door, entering a cinema and approaching the first girl in sight. His few pleasures were as regular as clockwork. Beware of dust in the mechanism, the unexpected that puts spice into life. He thought of the guards who had surrounded his villa since morning. This was the prison to which he would have to return. He got up with a sigh.

At the crossroads of the avenue Patrice Lumumba, a long line of cars was waiting. More identity checks? Who were they looking for? Dawad had triumphantly told him that they had found the authors of the tracts: a trio of activists who had already made a name for themselves. On seeing the Mercedes with the flag, the militia stood to attention after having roughly ordered the other cars to move over. Madou felt like asking them to go home and to give up this useless and unglorious job. He went by without saying a word, however, giving a vague Party salute to which they replied.

At the entrance to the grounds surrounding the Party's villa the two guards stood to attention as one man, holding their machine guns upright. Did they really know how to use them? It was common knowledge that the police, like the army, was incompetent, but in such cases incompetence is doubly dangerous. There seemed to be a change of guard at the foot of the steps – or that was the impression he got from the shouts, the comings and goings of a bus in the garden and the click of arms. To avoid any further standing to attention, Madou hurried up the steps. The main salon where he received visitors was empty, decorated with fresh flowers in a disorderly, arty arrangement. One of the countless boys placed at his disposal rushed in and, before dismissing him for the night, Madou asked him to bring something to drink. Some alcohol, which was unusual. At that moment, Zek was probably imbibing a considerable amount with a number of friendly hands on his shoulder. Tonight Zek had good reason to do so, and Madou envied him.

He went back on to the verandah. In the next-door villa some members of the delegation were indulging in their nightly orgy and making a din. On seeing Sali, Madou, who was no moralist, gave a friendly wave of complicity. He was momentarily tempted to join them. Then rejected the thought as improper. Not tonight, when Marie-Hélène was suffering and risking her life. Risking her life? Nobody died in childbirth nowadays. But he shivered, and imagined her cold and lifeless on a hospital bed. He went back into the salon and poured himself out another drink. If this continued he would be drunk before the night was over and he would not even have the excuse of celebrating fatherhood.

Without thinking, he pushed open the door of the room where he worked, and had barely entered when he came face to face with a young man who seemed to come out of the wall. He stared at this thin, rather dirty stranger with an oddly haggard, determined look. Was it somebody hiding there to ask him something?

'Who are you? What do you want?' he said, as gently as he could.

The stranger did not answer, and Madou realised he was paralysed with a fear that widened his irises and pinched the sides of his nose, making him look as if he were in a trance. Madou hated arousing fear.

'Come on, tell me what you want. I'm not going to eat you,' he repeated kindly.

The young man decided to speak.

'I've come to ask you about Muti,' he stammered. 'She's my mother's sister.'

Muti?

Madou had almost managed to forget her. How easy it was! He had pushed her shamefully to the back of his mind where he hoarded bad thoughts, recollections of cowardice and remorse. He had convinced himself that he had acted for the best, and that in the end he would ask for leniency from Toumany for an old woman who had yielded the names of his worst enemies. Her confession would surely be considered a change of stance, a new awareness, and she would be included in the first batch of political prisoners they would liberate in the promise made to Lopez de Arias. Therefore he was annoyed at hearing a name he had buried in oblivion being raised again.

'I have nothing to tell you on the subject,' he replied arrogantly. 'Get out or I'll call the guards.'

The young man then made a strange, convulsive movement and delved his hands way into the depths of his baggy trousers. He drew out a revolver and Madou stared in astonishment at this gleaming, well-oiled gun that seemed totally incongruous in his thin, still adolescent hand. It was as if he had been dragged to a stupid play whose characters were just as false as the situations in which they found themselves.

'Put that gun away', he said irritatedly, 'and get out of here. I have nothing to say to anyone.'

Zek got up. He had not drunk a drop of alcohol. Just when he was about to drink from his glass, the beer had changed into a sort of greenish bile and he had put his glass down in disgust. The familiar faces of his drinking mates had changed into grimacing masks. It was like once when he was a child. He had been with his uncle to a mask ceremony that women could not attend. It was a great honour, they told him, and with beating heart, he clutched his uncle's hand. The ancestor Dissiguibe, who had not appeared for a generation, would come out that day, and everyone was waiting for him with emotion and respect on the little square in Asin. The other masks had already started to dance between the huts' freshly-daubed walls and their new thatched roofs. The drums were beating. Suddenly a great voice sopke out and Zek had been scared to death. A malicious, expert hand had tied his insides in a knot and he had just had time to step away from his uncle before throwing up all the contents of his stomach over his beautiful, brand new, richly-embroidered *boubou* that Sokambi had slipped on him that morning as she lectured him as to how he should behave like a man. He couldn't remember what had happened after that. All he recalled was the shame he had felt that evening in front of Malan, his father.

Now he felt the same fear. His wife, his wife was in danger. She was going to leave this world without knowing how much she meant to him, without hearing all those things he had been unable to say to her throughout those long years together. What would his life be without Marie-Hélène? Like all the men of his ethnic group, Zek had been brought up with a kind of fear and contempt of women – malevolent creatures whose dark instincts had to be mastered. Love had taken him by surprise. He had difficulty accepting the power Marie-Hélène held over him and was convinced that no other man except him had undergone such humiliation. He remembered how his father had treated women like a herd of beggars. He especially recalled his way of treating Sokambi, his mother, whose cooking and body he had refused. She had never uttered a word. What was it that the men of that generation had had, which had now been lost?

He got into his car and roared off towards the hospital. At the Timbotimbo crossroads some militia tried to stop him.

'My wife's having a baby!' he yelled – or thought he yelled – gesticulating wildly.

Rihata's hospital did not look much. It was just a humble building of bricks and worm-eaten wood, standing behind weed-infested flower beds, and yet it was the best medical centre in the region. They owed it to a team of Polish doctors, sent by their country after independence, who had fallen in love with these polite, unfortunate people. Toumany's excesses had long since exasperated the Polish Government who recalled its expatriates. Those who remained behind lived off poverty-line wages. Indifferent to material comforts, they had remained in Rihata, often lacking basic drugs, giving free medical care, researching into pharmacopoeia and the plants used by the Ngurka medicine men, loved and respected by all. Thanks to them, the inhabitants of Rihata often said, while nodding their heads, 'Not all the Whites are bad, you know.'

Zek parked his car on the pavement and as he leapt out of it, almost knocked over two pretty nurses whom he would normally have noticed. The maternity ward was particularly old and cluttered, since the Polish doctors had nothing against the customary practice of having half the family staying with the patient. Apart from the wards, where there was suffering, births and sometimes deaths in the stifling promiscuity, there were two private rooms reserved for VIP wives. In fact, they were always empty. For the sake of prestige, the VIPs sent their wives to N'Daru, to clinics where medical treatment cost a fortune. Zek rushed to the labour room, also reserved for the élite, where he had left Marie-Hélène a few hours before. They pointed to room number two. Once in front of the blue, scratched door Zek felt his courage fail him. It was the first time the birth of one of his children had put him in such a state. Usually, while waiting for the fateful moment, he drained endless glasses in manly fashion and joked, glanced from time to time at the clock, then casually went to lean over the cradle. He usually kissed Marie-Hélène on the forehead. 'Another girl!' he would joke. 'Is that all you can produce? At least the granaries will be full!'

Why this unusual terror?

He tiptoed in, as if he wanted to make his enormous frame as small as possible. Marie-Hélène was lying on her side, apparently asleep. It was hot in the little room, which of course was not air-conditioned, and a window had been opened on to a flame tree loaded with pods. In a corner, a browned mirror reflected the paint flaking off the building opposite. Like a velvet jewel box, this humble setting contained everything that was most precious to him. He went over to the bed and Marie-Hélène opened her eyes. A smile he had not seen for years parted her lips and she was suddenly twenty years younger. In a flash of intensity he relived the first time he had seen her in the courtyard of the Sorbonne, a woollen hat perched on her lovely hair, a long scarf around her neck, and he had followed her bewitched to the Richelieu amphitheatre. He sat down next to her and placed a hand awkwardly on her cheek. Her smile widened.

'Have you seen him? He's the handsomest little thing!' she said in a weak, sleepy voice.

'Him?'

She nodded, and closing her eyes she smiled again as if she wanted to enjoy the trick she had just played on him.

'Yes. It's a boy.'

'A boy?'

It was then that Zek realised how much he had wanted a boy, how it pained him not to have one and how the birth of sons in his friends' families had seemed cruel and unfair. He had always smiled so much to hide his disappointment that he thought he had mastered it. He had joked and joked.

Now he was looking at this healthy baby with a thick mop of black hair and a curvy, sulky mouth like his mother's, and an almost lyrical song came to his lips. 'I shall name thee Elikia, which means "hope", since I have waited so long for thee. Thou shalt lead the way in the crowd and I shall recognise thee by thy little shaven head. Thou shalt be the palm tree in my desert, fresh water for my thirsty mouth. When my teeth have become useless thou shalt chew my kola nut so that I can recover my strength. At the journey's end thou shalt roll up my prayer mat after having closed my eyes. Elikia, yes, I shall call thee Elikia.'

He made a host of resolutions. Now that he had a son he would no longer drink. His son had no need for a druken father. He would be faithful to his wife. His son had no need for an adulterous father. Or for a pen-pusher. He would reach for the stars, the moon and the sun. He stood up, dazzled by his brilliant future. He returned home as if in a dream, laughing out loud at how surprised the children and Sokambi would be. At last, Sokambi would have her dream fulfilled. A son!

He was surprised to see a small crowd gathered in the garden. Had they already heard the news? Had they already come to congratulate him? The worried faces that turned to him, however, brought him down to earth.

156

Régis Antoine came up and took him by the arm. 'They've just killed your brother, Zek. They've shot the Minister.'

THIRTEEN

But Madou was not dead. After Victor had fired four bullets, he had been surrounded without offering any resistance and dragged off brutally to a waiting police van. The first bullet had lodged in Madou's left collar bone, the second had perforated his lung, the third had passed within inches of his heart, causing the most serious damage, and the fourth had lodged itself in the wall. He was lying in his mother's womb, far from the sound and the fury that the assassination attempt had triggered. He had not experienced such peace and quiet for a long time. He had returned to a time before childhood, before the creation of the world, before desire and sin. It was Eden.

The entire team of Polish doctors had been rushed in and was leaning over the operating table in the cold, shadowless light. In the corridor the delegation huddled together; some members held their heads between their hands, others called on God and fingered their beads, which had not been used for years. Others were bent on revenge and destruction. This small town would go down in history as another Sodom, punished for its sin down to the fourth generation. Ten telegrams and as many telexes had left for N'Daru. Against the advice of the doctor, Sali had first requested a special plane to take Madou back to the capital. Then he had demanded the top surgeons including the American who, the year before, had operated on one of Toumany's wives. He was now talking of calling the White House and the Elysée, but all the lines were engaged and it was impossible to get through.

Dawad and Nouram were busy on the job. The arrest by the guards of the wretched, half-stunned assassin was but the beginning. This attack could only be the result of a vast plot, as evidenced by Sory's song, the incidents at the Party youth section's show and, before that, the attack on Inawale, which they thought they had punished by arresting Muti. The ringleaders had to be found. Men and women were dragged from their beds, struck with rifle butts and led away to trucks tucked in the shadows and then to the hell of the prison cells. Never had the town's police stations and the sleepy prison – which only contained three common law offenders accused of having looted a market – been so crowded in one night. Identity checks were doubled and roads blocks set up at every crossroads so that the terrified locals no longer dared go out. The beggars and the homeless, who usually slept around the mosque or under the market lean-to roofs, went knocking on doors to ask for shelter in the name of Allah. They were seldom refused. Ibra was not surprised when he heard a knock on his door. Ever since the look Dawad had given him the day before, he knew the moment would come. He had just got married and turned to his young wife who was in tears. 'Go back to your parents tomorrow morning. Who knows when you'll see me again.'

Then he stepped out into the night. A few hours previously these militiamen had been his friends. They were of the same school. Now he had become a suspect – worse, a culprit – designated by Dawad as a scapegoat. He climbed into the van where about twenty people were already huddled, smelling strongly of suffering and fear. As he made his way across the jumble of half-bent legs a voice murmured, 'Ibra, they got you as well?'

He recognised Harouna, a young primary-school teacher and friend of Falade, which was probably his only crime.

The yard of the main police station had been quickly fenced off into two. The women were thrown to the right and the men

159

to the left. By morning, however, they had arrested so many men that they did not know where to put them, and stuck them with the women. Brothers, sisters and cousins were therefore reunited which brought some relief in the extreme chaos.

Surrounded by their right-hand men, Dawad and Nouram were holding a council of war. All were of the same opinion. The attack against the Minister should not only be used to rid them of their enemies and trouble-makers. That was short-term work. The opportunity should be taken to draw Toumany's attention to the region, and consequently to its officials, by demonstrating the efficiency of the repression and the fast, pitiless way in which it had been conducted. He must be forced into saying: 'These are clever men I've got here, who deserve more than their present jobs.'

Nouram already saw himself as chief of police in N'Daru. Dawad, who did not like the capital, saw himself as governor of the region, virtually equal to a minister. He would no longer have to bow down to men twenty years his junior. There was one point on which they did not agree – the number of arrests. Dawad thought the more suspects were taken to N'Daru the better. Nouram distrusted this simplistic reasoning. In his opinion the suspects should be selected. The people's tribunals that would probably be set up should not be given bleating victims likely to inspire pity in even the hardest of hearts. He was sorry that the assassin was not cynical and arrogant, and that after his crime he had turned into a frightened child.

Now that he had been thrown into the main police station cell from which Sory, Falade and his two companions had been removed, Victor was unable to accept what he had done. He recalled Madou's look of total incomprehension when he had fallen, the blood that had slowly dyed his clothes like a sacrificial animal's and the hoarse, muffled cry that had filled the room. When he had been in the northern territories he had seen the same sad dignity in cows as they were slaughtered.

'I have not brought about justice. I'm an executioner like them,' he repeated to himself with his head between his hands.

Surely killing was the greatest of crimes? What fate was in store for him? Why hadn't they battered him to death in the van that stank of urine, between the Party villas and the main police station? They probably wanted to make an example out of him. They would publicly hang him or cut off his head in N'Daru and the women would murmur ritual prayers half in pity, half out of liking for blood. Teresa, what would become of Teresa? She would forget him, that's all. Women are like that. Another man would give her a child, plant the son he had never had time to plant and she would offer up her sagging breast.

And his comrades back in camp, what would they think of him? Would they consider him a traitor for setting himself a solitary mission and carrying it out without orders? Without thinking of the consequences for the others? Or would they look on him as a hero? Would prayers be recited under the tents, words of gratitude and admiration be given for Ali Kerala, known as Victor, twenty-two years old? Would he become a martyr whose exploit would be sung for generations to come?

> *He set out alone,*
> *Alone,*
> *Life and death are our travelling companions,*
> *They fight each other*
> *Like the water fighting the earth.*

After all, what did it matter? Traitor, hero or martyr, he would be dead and know nothing about it.

What these locked up men and women did not know was that in a flash Rihata had become the capital of the land. Planes constantly landed and took off at the small airport. First the journalists started pouring in from *Falala*, the only daily newspaper, and then from the radio and television, with microphones, tape recorders, sound booms and cassettes. Passers-by would be asked what they thought of this horrible crime and they would stammer out an answer.

161

Then doctors of every nationality arrived, sent by Toumany, carrying heavy rectangular bags. Last of all came the fetish priests, who were kept at a distance by the team of Polish doctors. They nevertheless said prayers and made sacrifices under the trees of the enclosure, turning their faces to the ward where Madou was lying. The crowd of vagabonds, who had been camping under the windows since the attack, chanted and joined hands with them. They had great admiration for Saletigui who had predicted the fall of Kwame Nkrumah and been rewarded for his pains by a term in prison. The arrival of Madou's wife and her mother, her sisters, friends and servants took everyone's breath away. They had had no idea she was so young, not yet twenty, and so pretty, while her mother's regal expression gave her the dignity they had expected in Toumany's favourite niece. All these beautiful people piled into the Party villas, from which the less important delegates had been hastily driven and rehoused in the *lycée's* dormitories that had been given a quick clean. Rihata had never known such feverish activity. The Lebanese traders and market sellers tripled their prices, and there was a shortage of beer and whisky in the bars.

There was no doubt about it. It was Victor – thinner, uglier, with fear in his eyes and a pathetic gape. For a second, Varandio laid down his copy of *Falala* on his desk and was scared. Then he pulled himself together. Victor had spent one night at his house and had left at dawn, the hour of the first prayer. After all it was most unlikely that his neighbours had seen him. Masisi would not talk, since he had too much at stake as well. But in such cases you could never be too careful. He pressed a bell and Kali, his servant, came in with his usual frightened look.

'Go and get Teresa,' he ordered.

'The Portuguese woman, boss?'

That was what Kali and the rest of the household called Teresa, and suddenly Varandio realised how imprudent he had been. They would be sure to follow Victor's trail, discover he was with a woman, a 'Portuguese woman' and then who knows what would happen? As for Albert, the other companion, who had disappeared the day after Victor's departure, what had become of him? What was he going to do?

Teresa pushed open the door and her face needed no words.

'Have you heard the news?' Varandio managed to murmur.

She nodded. 'I listened to the radio yesterday evening.'

'Why did he do it? What was he hoping for? He's going to cause more harm than good.'

She did not reply and he got up as if standing gave him strength. 'Listen, you've got to leave.'

'Leave?'

'Yes, you must have friends, relatives or a family?'

'My family's on the other side of the river.'

'What can I possibly do for you? Go back to the north. You'll find your comrades.'

Victor had never said much to Varandio. But the latter had had no trouble guessing that he must have had links with the guerrillas. He also knew about Muti's activities in Farokodoba. He was already mixed up in that. There is a world of difference between alleviating the sad plight of political prisoners by circulating a few letters, and sheltering a killer.

'When do I leave?' Teresa asked softly.

'Immediately, now.'

Varandio hated having to act this way but he had no choice. He could see the inevitable, merciless repression that would clamp down on the country, the denunciations, acts of cowardice, retaliations and slander of every kind, weaving a venal web. He had a wife, three children and a successful career – even if he did hate it. Kali brought him his daily glass of iced grapefruit juice and he drank it slowly, without enjoying a drop. His mouth had a bitter taste of shame and remorse.

As he left the house Teresa set off as well, carrying a small bundle in her hand and wearing her headscarf down to her eyes. He avoided looking at her. He sat in the back of his car and pretended to be engrossed in *Falala* which he had already

163

read from cover to cover. The camp at Bafing was waking up. Soldiers in dark-green uniform headed for the training ground, while young recruits in shorts marched in step along the dusty tracks. The army was a huge, tentacular, cost-intensive body. Yet Varandio knew that only the officers enjoyed a privileged position. The regular, underpaid soldier, forced to do real hard labour building roads and bridges, clearing stones and draining marshes, remained in camp out of fear of an even greater wretchedness outside. Some of them, however, deserted and, according to Toumany, it was these bands of beggars who kept the rebellion going in the north. Why had Victor killed this Minister, one of the better ones in the Government? Madou had never been involved in a scandal and had come to negotiate a reconciliation which might have major implications for the regime. It was ridiculous. If he wanted to play kamikaze, why hadn't he emptied his gun into Toumany? At least he would have rid them of the stinking beast. All Victor had done was arm the repression. Varandio decided to interrupt his little humanitarian activities for a time. Even if cartloads of prisoners were brought to the camp he would keep low.

He got out in front of his office at the corner of the U-shaped construction that housed the camp's administration. He was in charge of transportation and he sighed at the thought of another sad day in front of him. A young soldier standing at the door gave him the Party salute which had replaced the military salute. 'Commanding Officer wants to see you.'

The Commanding Officer of the Bafing military camp, *Grand-Croix de l'Ordre National de la Panthère*, was also called Toumany. As there could not be two with the same name, they nicknamed him 'Homo', abbreviation for homonym, or 'Bata', which in Ngurka means second. He was a small, bouncing man with a loud voice, devastatingly intelligent and entirely devoted to evil. He had a craze for instruments of torture, sometimes inventing them, and delighted in trying them out on prisoners, surrounded by his close associates. He had little time for Varandio and his affected manner. He gazed at him critically. 'Varandio, if you were to pass an inspection, you would be told that your tie is not knotted according to regulations, your cap is not on correctly and your shoes are too pointed.'

Varandio pretended to laugh while the Commanding Officer's tone changed radically. He showed him the copy of *Falala* and three photos of Victor. 'Do you know this man?'

Varandio arched his eyebrows. 'I have never seen him in my life.'

'Are you sure?'

At the same time, Homo pressed a bell and Kali, the boy, appeared, eyes timidly to the ground.

'Tell us what you have to say.'

Kali was a very young man of eighteen or nineteen recently recruited by the army. He belonged to a despised ethnic group, the Sassama, who still lived half-naked in the forest to the west. Over the past few months there had been a major attempt at 'integrating and rehabilitating' them, the main reason being that the Minister for Culture's third wife was a young Sassama who had escaped the usual fate of her clan and had got a doctorate in marine biology from U.C.L.A. She could no longer put up with the contempt suffered by her own people.

Varandio was convinced he had always been good to Kali, leaving him abundant left-overs from his fine table, giving him cigarettes and once even lending him money to send a money order to his mother. Why such a denunciation? Then he realised that this simple, mystified soul believed he had to do his duty. When Kali had finished, Varandio shrugged his shoulders. He's made a mistake. Last week, a young cousin of my wife came and spent a few days with us. He looks a bit like this Victor.'

Homo smiled. 'Other members of your household have spoken. Don't force us to humiliate you in their presence. You will explain yourself to your peers.'

For a moment Varandio's mind was filled with wild thoughts. Draw his gun. Fire. Defend himself like a man.

What was the point? They would shoot him down like a dog. He might as well defend himself in front of a court. Defend himself? How many others before him had tried to defend themselves? With a kind of arrogance he threw his belt on to the desk.

They arrested Teresa, the 'Portuguese woman' in front of the cemetery. She was standing there with her head between her hands. She offered no resistance and admitted that Victor was her companion.

It was almost eleven when Marie-Hélène left the maternity ward and began pacing the grounds with her new-born son in her arms. Zek had promised to be there at nine, but his lateness, which in other circumstances would have exasperated her, left her indifferent. She did not pay any attention to the baby either. Usually she adored the moment when she finally took possession of her child. Up until that time the nurses, the paediatricians, the orderlies and the auxiliaries had come between the two of them. Suddenly they were alone, recalling those long months they had been together without ever seeing each other. That morning she could only think of Madou. She had only learned of the attack from Zek the day before, and had remained stupefied. Madou hurt, Madou in a coma – she could not believe it. He was there a few steps away in that modest ward and she could not go to him. She regretted their last incomplete meetings during which nothing had been said. Unfinished words. Embarrassed looks. Memories withheld. She refused to think he could die. Yet she surprised herself as she sifted through her memories like a miser counting his wealth. Memories which she had resolutely put out of her mind came flooding back.

When they had lived in N'Daru, they had taken advantage of Zek being away one weekend and had gone to the beach at Prahima. Oh, it had been nothing compared to the beaches in Guadeloupe! A meagre fringe of coconut palms crowned the dun-coloured dunes, covered with the remains of fish. Yet the sea had been wonderful. If you looked at it long enough it slowly lost its pale, slightly anaemic blue and turned green. And then an islet rose up out of the spray ...

The motor launch had been called *Esppère-en-Dieu*, but she had forgotten the name of the fisherman who, amid much swearing, had ferried them across. Their mother had never accompanied them. Official reason: she was a child from the hills and was afraid of the sea. Their father had never accompained them either. Official reason: business. So they would set off with three servants and Pierre, as naked as a little satyr. One of Siméon's sisters had lived there with a dozen chickens, as many rabbits and a dog called Balika. It was the only time they could escape from the Des Ruisseaux. Aunt Coralie, whom everyone called Man Keleman, had a large bosom in her loose-fitting dress and could not speak French. She treated her nieces like little princesses. Yes, in Prahima she had relived the delights of childhood.

When Madou took her by the hand she had felt she was capable of loving this land and putting down roots. She felt bitter now when she thought of what it could have been like and what Zek had not bothered to achieve.

Madou between life and death. Did she still love him? Why bother to ask? She had been happy with him, because of him, even if for the others her happiness had been a crime. It was unthinkable that he would die, that they would never see each other again and put right those last meetings. She was reminded of the baby by a weak gurgle and stroked his tiny fist. She asked him to forgive her for being so distant. They had a whole lifetime to get acquainted and to love each other. It was possible that Madou, who was lying in that small pavillion, did not have much longer to live.

They often used to go to the cinema, too. The films were not much and she could not remember any of them. But she had loved the ride through the town in its nocturnal frenzy. Hoodlums transformed by the night crowded in front of the discos; perverse yet childlike prostitutes wiggled inelegantly on the pavements, turning their painted faces towards the light of the bars. They had held hands with the innocence of children.

All these moments she had tried to forget were flooding back. He must not die. No, he must not die.

At that moment she saw Zek coming towards her followed by two of the beggars who frequented the neighbourhood of the hospital. He stopped to get rid of them by throwing them a few rais and, once again, she thought how much of the pharisee he had about him: 'God, I thank thee that I am more generous than other men.'

Where had it led them, his generosity? Come now, she was not going to sink into self-pity. She held it against Zek for being so naively happy to have a son and imagining that a male baby would wipe away years of misunderstanding, sulking and failure to communicate. She blamed him for feeling so little grief at Madou's attack and secretly considering it a just revenge of fate.

In fact, Zek was torn between conflicting feelings. Although the attack proved that nobody was invincible and had given Madou a good lesson, he did not want the outcome to prove fatal. What about his plans for the future? The visit to the *marabout* had cost him thirty thousand rais, part of which he had borrowed from his mother. Now that he had a son, he would have to change his life and make something of himself. He remembered how proud and happy he had felt when at every ceremony he had looked at his father, sitting in the front row of dignitaries, draped in a heavy woven toga with a chieftain's sandals on his feet. Founder of the first planters' union in the country, perhaps in all West Africa. And yet illiterate! Having all his correspondence written by a young primary-school teacher. What sort of mettle had the man been made of? He had listened in earnest to the applicants who constantly filed into his compound. At mealtimes there had been no counting the number of parasites who appeared from every corner of the village and made the women grumble. He should have lived then. When a man relied on his personal assets and not on intrigues, relations or his wife's family connections with Toumany. This brought him back to Madou. No, he certainly did not feel happy about his

168

condition. He did not want him to die, God forbid the thought. But he was not unhappy to see him learn at his own expense that the regime was hated throughout the country. There was not a word of truth in the official version of this counter-revolutionary plot designed to block the Government's process of liberalisation. Liberalisation or hoax?

He walked towards Marie-Hélène thinking how lovely she was with her figure back to normal; how attractive women were when they breast-feed. Whether she liked it or not she was his wife and nothing would prevent him this evening from reminding her of it. Besides, he knew her well enough to know she would not need reminding. He took the baby in his arms and to annoy her, said jokingly: 'I'm sorry, Muti, I was held up at the office.'

How poignant! Marie-Hélène realised in amazement that the attack on Madou gave Rihata a fairground atmosphere. Never had there been so many people strolling the streets or sitting on the terraces of the two or three pavement cafés. Small-time traders took advantage of this unexpected tourist boom to sell local crafts: river clay statuettes, reed mats and raffia tapestries, while the Lebanese traders put on show all the bric-a-brac and stuff they had had trouble selling. Suddenly Zek put his hand on hers. 'There is one visit we have to make this afternoon. His wife is here with his mother-in-law.'

For a moment, Marie-Hélène did not understand. She had never thought of Mwika, Madou's wife, since he himself seemed to attach so little importance to her. Suddenly she came to life. But curiously Marie-Hélène felt no jealousy towards this unknown girl who was young enough to be her daughter, and whom fate had dealt such a hard blow. What did she know of her husband's past? Probably nothing.

The children were waiting impatiently in the garden for their darling little brother whom only Christophe and Sia had been able to see at the hospital. But they were beaten to it by Sokambi who had abandoned her daily job of dyeing *pagnes* and was dressed in a sumptuous costume to welcome her first grandson. What was this power the birth of a male child had over these people? Marie-Hélène, who was only sporadically possessive, delivered up Elikia to his grandmother. The neighbours were already coming to the gate, anxious to welcome this seventh child, first son, who would surely have a brilliant future. A future minister? Why not a future president? They peered into his adorable little face as he lay fast asleep.

Once all the customary compliments had been made, the guests turned to the subject of conversation that could be heard all over town: the attack on the Minister. Zek noted with some annoyance that nobody contested the official version, the counter-revolutionary plot, and Madou from his bed took on the figure of a liberator and martyr. Régis Antoine, who up until then had ridiculed the pseudo-reconciliation, vehemently defended it. Who, until Madou, had bothered to moderate the whims of Toumany and introduce a little humanity and justice in his behaviour? Nobody, nobody. What about the opposition? They were made up of exiles who sat drinking in their Paris homes before going out to dance with local blondes. The assembly joined in unison. How illogical they were! Zek was tempted to reply that, if Madou were the victim of counter-revolutionaries bent on blocking liberalisation, it was very surprising that only progressives were being arrested who should be only too glad that things were opening up, and probably felt the changes were not fast enough. Then he decided against it. What would be the use? How easy it was to become a hero! All you had to do was die. With the bullets of a madman lodged in his body, Madou no longer represented the arrogance and arbitrariness of a hated regime. He had been given a new face. New features. Zek realised in disgust that whatever he did his brother would always be the winner. If he recovered from his wounds the whole country would persuade Toumany to propel him to the very top – unless he became peeved with his right-hand man's popularity and had him shot. Zek who had never had a head for politics, started imagining a thousand complex possible outcomes.

In the meantime, Marie-Hélène climbed the stairs

turning her back on the noisy assembly of visitors. In her opinion, all the events of African community life were devoid of meaning and paid lip-service to a past of which nothing was left. She was bored to death. The same greetings were recited every time. The same exclamations were made. The same jokes repeated. The same gestures. She knew nobody was shocked by her behaviour any more. For years they had been used to the strange habits of the 'foreigner'. In her room she scrutinised herself in the old wardrobe mirror. Still too much fat around her middle and thighs, but that would soon go. How wrinkled her hands were! And her neck had started to be the same. She could still make an impression. But she would shortly be one of those old wrecks about whom people would say, 'My God, she must have been lovely.'

The poison of old age was circulating in her veins.

If Madou died she would have no chance of leaving Rihata before it was too late, before her finest years had flown. Suddenly she began turning his attractive offer over in her mind, yet she was afraid it might be an act of pity. Zek, commercial attaché! She had no inclination to go back to Paris, but she had nothing against London, Montreal and New York, especially New York. They would be close to black people, close to their tragedies and mediocre victories. Olnel used to describe the city, and closing her eyes believed she was there. Harlem, the bleeding heart, the humiliated heart.

Then she regretted the selfish turn her thoughts were taking while Madou was dying. She had not prayed for years. She had not even prayed at Delphine's death. So how could she find the words now?

When there was a knock on the door she knew it was Christophe. She guessed what he must be thinking. Wouldn't this new-born son subtly remind Zek that Christophe was merely an illegitimate child admitted to the family out of indulgence? Perhaps soon made to feel out of place? She knew Zek well enough to know that such thoughts would never cross his mind. Christophe was his child, the only one he had chosen to have. He had been the first to love him and nothing was going to change that.

171

FOURTEEN

The line of cars moved off. Following a technique used for Muti's transfer to N'Daru, the main police station had asked the military camp in Bafing to help out. They had sent a dozen armed guards, three armoured Peugeot vans – like the one used for the old woman – and a small cell-like car reserved for reputedly dangerous prisoners. Qualified as an assassin, Victor was entitled to the latter, although everybody could not help feeling sorry for him. It was obvious he had been a mere executant. Those who had armed him were already a long way off. While awaiting confirmation of the official version that would come from Toumany himself, the journalists had already written their papers. Victor was depicted as a sad example of the manipulation to which young people were being submitted. Anxious to see the return of the white masters and the creation of a neo-colonial regime, these manipulators did not dare place themselves in the spotlight, but carried out their dirty business from foreign capitals, using simple, easily-influenced minds. The journalists wrote their reports even more freely since nobody had been admitted to interview the unfortunate Victor, who had been kept hidden since his crime. One of the reporters from *Falala* did receive information that repeatedly linked Victor to the guerrillas in the north, but since this movement only existed in enemy minds, how could it be published in the official daily?

Ibra, Sory, Falade and Harouna, plus dozens of others suspected of being accomplices and criminals after a hasty interrogation, were piled into the vans. The people's tribunals set up in N'Daru would discover the truth and inflict the necessary penalties. Sory understood nothing of what was going on. He could see no connection between his angry outburst of song the day his son was given a name, and this attack on a minister he had never met. Why were they taking him to N'Daru? He made great efforts to explain his case to everyone around him, but since nobody was in a mood to listen to him he wondered whether he was not dealing with brutes as selfish as those outside. After all, shouldn't his travelling companions have all shouted together, 'No, not Sory! Not Sory! He hasn't done anything.'

The presence of Ibra made his confusion complete. What was a member of the regional secretariat doing among this wretched lot? When he saw two guards administer him a series of kicks he wondered whether the earth was still round. It must have become diamond-shaped, out of the sun's reach.

He slumped back on to the hard, wooden bench. Beside him a young man, hardly eighteen, was sleeping with his mouth open, exhausted from hunger and fear. What was he accused of? Sory thought of his wives, and tears hardly worthy of a man came to his eyes. He had left them without a cent, since the money Zek had given him had scarcely covered the cost of the name-giving ceremony. What would they do with the kids? He pictured the face of his youngest son and a feeling of anger and revolt crept over him. If God existed these criminals who had torn a father from his family would be punished! God! It seemed he had uttered a word devoid of meaning. Then he was frightened of his blasphemy and tried to recite a ritual prayer.

Ibra, whose knees were digging Sory in the back, felt a crushing feeling of remorse. It seemed he was responsible for this man's arrest. Wasn't he one of those who had hired him, dangled a thousand promises in front of him and then not kept them? Sory had been earning his own living, like his father

173

before him. They had made a civil servant out of him. And now he was travelling to his death, which lay at the end of this road. The people's tribunals were composed of Party rogues or poor wretches prepared to convict father and mother for a handful of rais. Their verdict was predictable. Sometimes, Toumany treated himself to the luxury of pardoning a few criminals. Perhaps they would be lucky. But then what sort of life would they lead? Doors would be shut in their faces. They would wander like lepers ringing bells and make honest citizens run a mile to avoid them. At that moment he had a flash of inspiration and, leaning forward, he gently whispered, 'Sing, Sory, sing.'

The *griot* turned round and stared at him. He repeated the request and Sory slowly shook his head, clearly thinking this was a madman. Sing at such a moment!

Then, for some inexplicable reason, the other prisoners started repeating, 'Sing, Sory, sing' and the van filled with a muffled sound that ran from mouth to mouth. The guards on the other side knocked on the partition with their rifle butts to call for silence. But they did it half-heartedly as they were not totally impervious to emotion. They pitied these poor devils, some of whom were relatives and mirrors of their future fate. When their officers were absent they tended to be indulgent.

Sory was a born actor. His father and grandfather had been actors before him. His contact with others, their response and admiration, had always stimulated him and he could not let a leading role slip through his fingers. It was partly this which had led to his outburst of anger a few days earlier. If he had been left to himself he might not have had the strength to stand up in front of Dawad. This murmur around him had the effect of ointment for his wounds. These men knew him then? A kind of pride went to his head and he stared at Ibra again. 'You want me to sing?'

'We all want you to. Can't you hear?'

Yes, he could hear.

Sing. All right? But what? He thought a moment. Then, closing his eyes and throwing back his head, he thundered out the *Epic of Bouraina*. The beautiful song drifted through the armoured windows of the van and out into the countryside. For long after, the peasants lying on their mats talked of the spirits they had heard making such a din at midnight. The sound finally reached the head of the convoy and Victor, pricking up his ears, thought he must be hearing things. His companions were singing! Had they gone mad? Do sheep or cows on their way to the slaughterhouse suddenly decide to sing? He had no trouble recognising the *Epic of Bouraina*, the national Ngurka hero, known by all the children in the country. Bouraina, his father's seventh son, had to flee the kingdom after a quarrel with one of his stepmothers, unfortunately the old king's favourite wife. He set off into exile taking with him in a *pagne* a little of his native soil and some of his mother's smoked water-buffalo meat in a skin bag. After a long and difficult journey he and his followers reached a land approved by his fetish priests, when a group of Moslems stopped him and asked for the little food he had left. His companions, who were furious at the disrespect shown by these insolent Moslems to the young prince, wanted to kill them. Bouraina, however, refused and shared the contents of his bag. The Moslems, who were but spirits in disguise, predicted his future victories and told him how his kingdom would spread from the mountains to the sea. Yes, this country had been great! He had known other Bourainas and many other heroes. All the peoples who made up this country today had had their hour of glory and power.

So why did they tolerate domination? Where would the initial spark of anger come from? When would the revolt come? Could one ex-brigadier general put them in chains? But this one ex-brigadier general was not alone. He had half the governments of the world behind him. How could you fight them? Once again Victor was about to sink into despair when he was struck by a thought. Didn't the anger and the revolt already exist? Wasn't it already evident in a thousand ways? Sory's song, the tracts, the guerrilla warfare in the north, however feeble and isolated they were ... Suddenly he felt capable of taking responsibility for what he had done. No, he was not the executioner he had thought. He had done justice. Imperfect justice like all the rest. But justice all the same. Toumany had been deprived of one of his most dangerous lieutenants, who gave the regime the face of respectability. Victor saw Madou again as he had appeared to him during that one, crucial moment. Slim, distinguished and self-confident. One of those men about whom people said, 'He's different from the rest. With him about, things won't be the same.'

Their presence justified many a crime. He had done justice and revenged Muti.

Alone in his cell-like car, plunged in darkness, set on a course with the most sinister of fates, he too found the strength to sing the *Epic of Bouraina*.

Madou opened his eyes and found himself in a small, stuffy room with an enormous weight across his chest that prevented him from breathing. He was about to complain and ask to go back to where he had come from when a gentle hand stroked his forehead. A woman was sitting at his bedside. Surprised, he recognised Muti.

'How do you feel, son of Malan?'

Madou did not like being called son of Malan. Not because he was ashamed of his father, but because he considered himself an individual in his own right and such a name reduced him to nothing. Unlike Zek, who had no objection to stating his origins, he never spoke of his father who, in his own way, had been a great leader and militant. It is much nobler to be born from nothing and to climb the ladder alone. But no such protest came from his lips. He had to make the most of his unhoped-for meeting with the old woman, to try and explain himself and be forgiven. Madou collected his thoughts together.

'Listen to me Muti. I had no other choice. What did you expect me to do? Save the conspirators? How could I? Like the sun high in the sky, the eye of Toumany sees all that goes on in this country.'

Muti smiled indulgently. 'Forget all that. I believe you. You did what you could.'

'But you, I want to save you. I'll have you pardoned by Toumany.'

Speaking like this made the sweat stream down his forehead, and his chest hurt even more. Muti placed a finger on his lips.

'Hush. It doesn't matter any more.'

There was something in her size that reminded him of his mother, Aissa. When he was born, Aissa was no longer very young and had already had five children, but she had still been Malan's favourite because she was the only wife who sometimes consented to listen to him. She did not seem to share in the general adoration of Madou, and rebuked him severely for any weakness. He was no dupe. She wanted him to be perfect, superior in all ways to that dunce, Zek, who only knew how to kick a football around. She hated Sokambi and she had conveyed this feeling to her unfortunate son. When they were small, Madou and Zek managed not to get mixed up in their mothers' intrigues. It was afterwards that things had gone wrong. Afterwards ... where was Marie-Hélène? He groaned again when a voice, her voice, stopped him. 'I'm here, my love.'

He was surprised. Marie-Hélène was not a woman of tender words. Was he that ill?

Opening his eyes, he saw her next to Muti with the same sweetness and tenderness on her face. She had given birth at last. Her body was back to its former lovely shape and her ample breasts made her all the more beautiful. She smiled. 'We have a son. He's sleeping and you should be sleeping, too.'

He was a little surprised to hear that Marie-Hélène's son was his since he had not seen her for so long. But he did not dare contradict her and besides, this son replaced the other child she had never admitted was his. The only moments of happiness in his life had been when he was with her; of that he was sure. When he was nothing but a younger brother loaded with diplomas and looking for a job, Zek had suggested, 'You

177

ought to go and see Old Neboma. He was a good friend of father's and is respected in high places.'

Madou had shrugged his shoulders. He refused to kowtow.

'If you don't, you won't get anywhere,' Zek would say in a haughty tone, sipping his drink.

Well, he had not gone to see him, and he had got somewhere. Soon he would be Prime Minister. Wouldn't he? Marie-Hélène lent over and smiled again.

'What does it matter if you are Prime Minister. Aren't we happy being together?'

But that was just it; they were no longer together. They had been separated. His life had taken a turn for the worse after that rainy season when she had left Rihata with Zek, her children and the baby he thought might be his. He went round in circles in his tiny, three-roomed flat watching the rain, the mud and the children splashing in the puddles. These dismal surroundings seemed to sum up his future. Being singled out by Toumany, working at his side and taking on more responsibilities had been one way of escaping the terrible certainty that never again would he experience happiness, however much the envious men around him bowed down to him. He had done his best. With a group of men of his own age, sarcastically called technocrats by Toumany's old guard, he had tried to turn a new page. This reconciliation with Lopez de Arias was a prelude. Wasn't it a prelude?

'Yes, it's a prelude,' Marie-Hélène said, as if reassuring a child.

Prelude to happiness. The prison gates would stand ajar. A stream of emaciated wretches, almost unable to speak after so many years of silence, blind like Fily, would stare at the sun they had forgotten. Was this, then, the light of day? How good and comforting. Children would be reunited with their fathers, wives with their husbands – and all this would be his work. His work alone.

'How you fret. What's the use of thinking about all that?'

He would have liked to think of something else. Or simply of nothing at all. Return to the darkness and warmth in which he had wrapped himself earlier. But it was impossible. A cruel force had troubled his peace and kept him awake. Suffocating. Stifling. Muti and Marie-Hélène had departed, and despite his calls they did not return. In their place stood two bearded, blond-haired men who meant nothing to him. He stubbornly closed his eyes as if this would drive them from his bedside. 'We'll have to give him a tranquilliser,' a voice said.

And he remembered the first needle they had stuck in him as a boy at the clinic in Asin.

Marie-Hélène reappeared, but not alone. She was with Sia, her eldest daughter, who for the first time looked affectionately at her uncle – or father, the two words meaning the same in Ngurka. Why had she been so angry with him? She smiled, and he realised he had been mistaken. She had never stopped loving him. He would have liked to have explained what had happened between her mother and him, but she indicated that it was not necessary. She understood. Who had invented such horrible words as sin and adultery? The main thing was to be happy, and he had made Marie-Hélène happy. Thanks to him she had stopped torturing herself; she had forgotten Zek, his nightly absences and his infidelity. She had almost forgotten a past which he knew was a painful one and about which he did not ask. And he would make Sia happy too. He would take her to N'Daru. From the top of the highest building, the hotel *Impala*, he would show her the town, lying at her feet like a docile animal; the lagoon, like a mottled snake; the green and purple of the gardens and the constant stream of cars which came from every corner of the industrialised world. How far it had come in twenty years! A metropolis had replaced a village. Some people would try and point out the other side of the coin – the dismal shanty towns. However much he tried to chase them away, these images clung to him and swarmed around him in a sinister merry-go-round. He was responsible for it all. Him? Responsible? He began to gasp for breath and the blond men leant over him again, saying something he could not understand.

Then peace returned. Darkness closed in again, and a sort of coolness filled his veins.

Muti and Marie-Hélène stood by his bedside with a third

woman whose features he could not at first make out. It seemed that she was crying with her head between her hands. When she moved suddenly he recognised Mwika. Mwika, his child wife, so deprived of love, and whose warm, consenting body he suddenly missed. He had not made her happy. Not happy? Why? She had a Mercedes sports car, jewels worked by the best Senegalese craftsmen, woven cloth from Kumasi in Ashanti country, bags, shoes and perfumes from Europe. What more did a woman of her generation want? Born at the time of African independences, she had only learnt to appreciate material things. She was judged by her outward appearance. No, he was irreproachable as far as she was concerned. He had provided her with everything she needed to walk with head held high among her equals. Their son was handsome and had the self-assurance of a spoilt child. Hadn't he given her everything?

The bitter taste of blood filled his mouth as a harsh light invaded the room. In a nightmare he saw himself lying on a narrow bed with two drip feeds standing guard at his head. The bearded, blond-haired men were looking at each other and two women in white uniforms were staring at him, terrified. The walls of the room were white, too, but a dirty, yellow white. Someone had put red roses in a vase.

When the death of Madou was made public, Dawad and the members of the secretariat decreed regional mourning without awaiting orders from N'Daru. The national flag, red, green and yellow with a black sickle, was lowered to half mast on the few public buildings, and the shopkeepers in the rue Patrice Lumumba were asked to lower their metal blinds. The population of Rihata split into two clans. Those who had a relative or friend arrested and transferred to N'Daru, and who were of the opinion that the Minister should have gone and died elsewhere; and those who were touched by the death of a young man said to be destined for a brilliant future.

What makes things the way they are? If Madou had had a paunch and a leering face like so many of Toumany's

180

companions, perhaps there would have been fewer tears shed. But for the time being all they could remember, with a deep sense of injustice and regret, was his figure; and the grace with which he had stepped down from the plane.

When she heard the news, shortly after the first prayer, Elizia, Falade's wife, wrapped her head in Sawale headgear and left the compound with her youngest daughter on her back. She had not had time to weep since the moment when her husband had been arrested. There were reports which had to be sent to the somewhat absurdly-named organisation *Ordre Rouge* of which Falade and several other young people were members. These reports could not be sent through the post. They were relayed from village to village to N'Daru where the leaders were located. When she had first got married she wanted nothing to do with this *Ordre Rouge*. So Falade had 'educated' her, and now she was the one who could not wait for the radiant dawn he promised. They were the ones who had produced and distributed the tracts at the Party's youth section evening, but they had nothing to do with the Minister's assassination. Now that he was dead, what was going to happen? Was the repression going to get worse? When she arrived in front of Dr Faik's house she looked around carefully.

The inhabitants of Rihata called Dr Faik 'Dr 2CV' for this half-caste, who only had to say the word to take his place among the local dignitaries, drove around in a car that made the children split their sides laughing. It was not very prudent to come and see him on a morning like this since three of his nurses had been arrested, and the clinic he directed was, according to Nouram, a breeding ground for activists who were being kept under close watch. He expected to be arrested at any moment, but Elizia needed to talk and receive a little human sympathy.

Faik was sitting sadly at a table covered with a stained cloth. 'You've heard the news?' he murmured on seeing her.

She nodded.

'What's going to happen now?'

'Nobody knows. They have already arrested everyone who

181

could be arrested. Except me. We'll have to wait.'

Despite its name, the aims of the organisation were totally pacifist and consisted of literacy and information campaigns for the peasants. The anti-malaria rounds, the screening for parasites and the refresher courses for midwives provided the opportunity to make contact with thousands of men and women who were tired of poverty and ignorance. In the booklets produced by Falade and a group of primary school teachers, Marxism was hardly ever mentioned. They spoke of democracy, political parties and elections; words which in that country had lost their original meaning. That was already a crime! Elizia and the other members' wives had spent hours burning such documents in their outside stoves.

'So we don't do anything?'

'We become twice as vigilant.'

He lowered his voice. 'I have been told that this Victor is a guerrilla from the north ... not a counter-revolutionary.'

Elizia opened her eyes wide. A guerrilla? Where did he get this information from? Was it reliable? Or just the figment of overwrought imaginations, half-crazed by dictatorship?

Dr Faik shook his head. 'A lot of things are happening in this country, Elizia. Despite appearances, the days of Toumany are numbered.'

She had been hearing that for years.

Zek learned of his brother's death while he was shaving in the bathroom, listening to his transistor radio. He stood staring stupidly at his face in the mirror. Then he switched off the radio and pictures crowded his mind. Madou as a puny little boy crying for a slice of the green mango he had just picked. Madou accompanying him to the soccer ground and clapping with all his might when he scored a goal. Madou in his khaki college uniform, his baggy shorts above his big, scuffed, scarred knees, wearing the expression of intelligence and arrogance that was never to leave him. Madou returning from Russia and capturing the heart of Marie-Hélène. Madou struck down in the bloom of his youth, the sap of life dribbling down his sides. He thought he had hated his brother. He probably had. Yet at that moment he was immensely saddened that Madou would never achieve what he had set out to do, and that his life would always have an unfinished taste about it. The Polish doctors had prevented him from seeing Madou at the hospital. So what would be the last picture he would have of him? Without knowing why, he selected one like choosing a set of prints from a photographer. Madou stepping out of the presidential plane, slowly raising his fist above his head, then nimbly descending the gangway. Madou victorious, now that he was nothing. Then he thought of Marie-Hélène, and how he would announce the news to her. By a quirk of fate he was no longer the outraged and offended husband, but a living person speaking of a dead one, and who could afford now to be indulgent. Forgiving and forgetting.

He turned out the light, crossed the room where Marie-Hélène was still sleeping and went out on to the balcony. He saw Sokambi in the garden, kneeling on her mat, busy with her first prayers. The news had been announced in every language; she could not have failed to have heard it. What was she feeling? You could no longer hate someone who was dead.

Madou was dead. So that meant that life was not going to change. There would always be the same sky over his head, the same office at the bank, the same drinking partners at the *Nuit de Sine* before going home to increasingly unsatisfied children and an ageing wife as sour as whey. He was ashamed of his thoughts. And yet he could not help thinking angrily of the sheep he had sacrificed, a symbol of all the hopes that had suddenly been aroused in him. He took hold of himself and went back into the room. Marie-Hélène was asleep, lying on her stomach, her face pressed against her bent arms. All he could see was her mass of hair with its familiar perfume. He put his hand on her shoulder and she slowly recoiled like she did whenever she had finished making love with him, when she went back to being distant or openly hostile. He shook her impatiently. How could she sleep at such a time? There is said to be an intuition which signals a natural communion with a beloved one who has departed. Hadn't she felt or realised anything in her sleep? A man who had adored her, made love to her and recently been concerned with her future, had left this life. And that had not disturbed her dreams?

How like a woman to be so selfish and callous.

Marie-Hélène finally opened her eyes and sat up against her pillows.

'What a dream I've just had,' she murmured in a melancholy voice.

About time! About time!

'A dream?' Zek asked gently, easily won over to pity.

But she remained silent, as if she could no longer recollect the horror and terror she had felt. He took her hand which had started to wrinkle; in places her lovely light-brown skin had yellowed and the veins had swelled.

'Be brave, my love, he's dead,' he whispered.

Then he drew her against him, because he did not want to see the tears which might make it harder for him to forgive and forget.

Meanwhile, Christophe had gone into the room that Sia shared with Alix. The two girls were still asleep and all he could make out was a mass of tangled hair, arms, slender legs and the contour of a buttock that he irritatedly covered up. He shook Sia, who opened her eyes and angrily gave him a kick. This was no time for games.

'Sia, he's dead,' he murmured. 'They've just announced it on the radio. He's dead, Sia.'

She stared at him in silence for so long that he wondered whether she had understood.

'Does *Maman* know?' she asked.

He thought the question quite incongruous and shrugged his shoulders. She got up, slipped on the pretty raffia slippers edged in red which she had received at Christmas, and headed for the door, while Alix, now awake, repeated mechanically, 'Who's dead, Christophe? Who's dead?'

184

Sia could only think of her mother. The conjectured liaison that had so disgusted her became a secret between the two of them and brought them closer together, uniting them in a new-found intimacy. Nobody would really know what this death meant to Marie-Hélène. She received the ritual condolences. According to Ngurka tradition, Madou, as her husband's brother, was entitled to the same name and she was entitled to the ritual chant:

The stream crosses the path,
The path crosses the stream,
Which is the older of the two?
Mother of sons, mother of sons,
Your husband has gone to cut wood
And has not returned.

But they did not know the actual extent of her grief. How illogical life was! If Zek had been the first of the two brothers to die, his widow would have gone to his younger brother. Then what had once been a crime would have been given everyone's blessing.

Zek stood on the balcony like a punished child and Sia realised that Marie-Hélène had sent him out so that she could cry in peace.

'Don't disturb your mother, she's sleeping,' he stammered, and made as if to stop her going in.

Sia went in regardless. She could only feel nauseated when she entered this big, sparsely furnished room because it was impossible not to imagine what happened at night on the large bed covered with a faded Indian bedspread. Given her age, Sia could not comprehend that the sexual act was not necessarily an act of love. Her parents, therefore, seemed monstrous to her. But at that moment her thoughts were not on judging, but consoling. While her mother was crying shamelessly into her rumpled nightdress, double-edged in lace around the collar and cuffs and giving her the look of an overgrown boarding-school girl, she noted the silver streaks in her hair, the first wrinkles on her forehead, the loose flesh around her shoulders and neck, and the slight droop of her breasts swollen with the milk which would soon be guzzled by Elikia. She realised that Marie-Hélène was irrevocably saying farewell to her youth, to courtship, to making mistakes – or even committing sin – to inflicting pain, on others and herself. Henceforth, she was going to venture into the great desert of middle age and cross this Sahara of memories and regrets without a guide. Tears came to Sia's eyes while a prayer she could not repress went over and over in her mind. 'Please God don't let my life be like hers.'

At the same time she recalled what Madou had promised her: holidays in N'Daru with the elegant young set, so different from the bush people of Rihata, who would open their Porsche doors for her and describe the skyline of Manhattan where they had spent the previous season. The music from the bars, throbbing like drums, and the lamps on the bridge over the lagoon. All those promises that would never be kept. Never. Never. Never.

FIFTEEN

Toumany, historical leader and president for life, commonly known as the 'Supreme Helmsman', 'Roof of the World' or 'Father of Sons', looked up in tears at his secretaries. 'He's dead! He's dead!'

The secretaries did not say a word; little was said in front of Toumany, and they usually only spoke when told to do so.

'I decree a national mourning of forty days,' he continued, gasping for breath. 'Schools, ministries and state shops will be closed. Bring his body back as quickly as possible. He will have the funeral he deserves: the police, the army and my personal Leopard-guards. Tonight, I'll go on television to speak about him.'

Then he stood up and began to stomp around the room with a left leg that had rotted in a swamp in Indo-China while he was a soldier. Yes, his pain was sincere. He had slept badly, too, because his teeth were giving him trouble again. For two years they had been rotting in his gums and his American stomatologists had had no other choice but to pull them out one by one and replace them with bits of porcelain. Porcelain? What next! He had more faith in the fetish priests who saw his enemies at work – mainly those who had given up hope of bringing Fily back to power – and treated him with a mixture of menstrual blood, the froth of male toads, orchid pollen, baobab leaves, beeswax and *lagerstroemia speciosa*.

This mixture of grief and minor complications was the last straw. Having written everything down on large notepads, the secretaries waited for further orders that soon came.

'I want to see Umaru, Minister of Defence and Security, Bugana, Minister of the Interior, and my friend Moshe. Immediately. Go and carry out your orders.' The little group of men rushed out.

Toumany had loved Madou as an ageing man loves a young man, an ugly man a charmer, and a lecher an ascetic, indifferent to women and alcohol. He had never really understood why Madou had served him, and the attachment of such people made him think his power less hateful. With his hands clasping his head he remained standing in front of one of the windows that looked out on to the two hundred and fifty acre park surrounding his castle at Reduasi. Through the trees he could see the scarlet uniforms of his Leopard-guards, machine guns at the ready. It was time for the changing of the guard. During an official visit to Great Britain he had been so impressed by the ceremony at the gates of Buckingham Palace that he had reproduced the ritual step by step. Usually he never tired of watching it, but today it left him indifferent.

Madou was dead! Madou, who had provided him with all he needed to rid him of his enemies. The clear, detailed reports he had sent on Muti's confessions had found their way to two allied embassies which were already in consultation on how to act. With a little luck they would finally crush the guerrilla movement in the north. At the meeting of the National Opposition Front arranged by these fools, they would strike down the leaders in one go. They would have all their eggs in one basket. They would be smashed and their shells scattered to the wind. Toumany laughed out loud. Not in fun. In cruel derision.

At this moment a servant entered, carrying a magnificent tray with all the sweetmeats usually ordered by the 'Supreme Helmsman' for his breakfast. In his present mood nothing found favour in his eyes, and he only kept the Louis XIV style coffee-pot full of ink-coloured liquid which he had learnt to appreciate during a private visit to Haiti, where the dictator was one of his personal friends.

He clapped his hands to call Kunene, his latest wife, still fast asleep in the next room. She finally emerged in her dark-red brocade dressing gown. In actual fact, Kunene had been the fiancée of his sixth son. When Toumany had seen her at last ceremony commemorating the *coup d'état*, he had fallen madly in love with her. So he had paid her parents a handsome dowry, while his son went to join his elder brothers who were plotting to overthrow their father in foreign capitals, from time to time giving exclusive interviews to left-wing journals. Yes, he had loved Madou. Like a father disappointed with his own sons. Like a protector betrayed by his protegés, who found nothing better to do than slander him. Like a lover deceived by his mistresses.

'Massage me, my little kitten,' he ordered Kunene after his fourth cup of coffee. 'I ache all over.'

Kunene obeyed, her mind on other things. She had received a letter from Madhi, her former fiancé, begging her to come to her senses and join him in Abidjan, from where they would fly to Spain. As her deft hands neared the withered sexual organs of her old husband, whom she had accepted through greed, he trembled and took her in his arms. So Moshe, Umaru and Bagana had to kick their heels in the ante-room while the 'Supreme Helmsman' made love.

Toumany first of all saw Moshe, the director of the sinister PPM police force. He was one of his oldest friends. They had been cadets together, prisoners during the Second World War and escapees from Indo-China. While the leg of one rotted in a swamp, the other got a shell splinter in his right eye and had to wear a black leather eyepatch like Moshe Dayan, hence his nickname. Moshe looked worried and refused the cup of coffee that Toumany offered him. Their long friendship meant that he did not have to wait for the 'Supreme Helmsman' to speak first.

'Boss, I almost came to see you yesterday. I have received a very interesting piece of information.'

'About what?'

Moshe took a little snuff and lowered his voice. 'One of my relatives brought a certain Sadan to me, the police chief in Rihata where Madou was killed. A man you can really trust who told me his suspicions about a prisoner, a certain Muti.'

Toumany burst into a laugh that surprised even Moshe.

Muti! May she return to her mother's wretched womb, which she should never have left! Don't say any more, I know all about her.'

Moshe was surprised. 'How's that?'

Toumany laughed even louder. 'Before he died, Madou – my spiritual son, may he rest in peace, may his soul soon be reincarnated in the body of a male child – told me everything about her in his reports. The mad old woman supposedly confessed to him.'

Moshe gestured philosophically. So Sadan had made the journey from Rihata to N'Daru for nothing and could not hope for any reward. Toumany got up and assumed a solemn look. 'Muti's head will not be the only one to roll in the dust. I want you to interrogate all of those who were involved in some way or another in the death of my spiritual son. I want thorough, detailed confessions. The people's tribunals will do their duty. They know how to carry it out. Public executions, naturally!'

Moshe, who hated Madou, said nothing. He was not unhappy that this young whelp, who treated everyone with contempt and cut the ground from under their feet, had been given a good lesson, and had learnt to his cost that misfortune and death turn up unannounced. Then he stood up. 'You can count on me,' he said, soberly.

When he left, Toumany did not have Umaru or Bagana shown in. He remained plunged in thought. In reality, this feigned reconciliation with Lopez de Arias, who had so humiliated him in the past, was but a manoeuvre. By seeming to veer to the left, he simply wanted to frighten his good friends and guarantors who had started to fill his head with talk of human rights, and wanted to dispatch a horde of IMF experts to take over the country's shaky economy. He would no longer be master in his own house! Had the Whites been driven out twenty years ago for that? Not for one second had Madou managed to convince him of the need to liberalise the regime. Obviously, Madou had not suspected anything, otherwise he would not have put so much heart into the job. His assassination now added to the apparent authenticity of his undertaking. The effects were already being felt and friends were wondering whether he had not gone further than they thought along the road to reconciliation, negotiation and a change of tack. They were now prepared to grant him the loans they had been refusing. With no strings attached! Toumany laughed out loud. The world was one gigantic safe. All you needed to do was find the combination.

So his debt to the departed Madou was twofold. The destruction of his most implacable enemies and the rapprochement with his defaulting, yet remorseful allies. He recalled Kunene, who had started to doze off again in a neighbouring room, and came back looking annoyed. 'Listen my little kitten. What if I named him Prime Minister posthumously?'

Kunene yawned behind her ringed hands. 'Who? Madou? What's the use of a posthumous Prime Minister?'

'None whatsoever! But that way we won't have to appoint another!' They looked at each other and she could not help bursting out laughing at the sight of her sly old husband. Dear old Toumany. It wouldn't be that easy to get the better of him.

191

Glossary

accra heavy, batter cod fritters

awele traditional African game played with cowries

balafon traditional African xylophone made from calabashes

beguin French Caribbean dance

boubou full, loose tunic worn by men and women

grimauds/grimelles a category of half-caste in the West Indian
    colour system

griotte poet, musician, praise singer

kora traditional African stringed instrument

marabout Moslem holy man

mariachis traditional Mexican musician

pagne wrapper of loose cloth worn by both men and women